A Family for Thanksgiving

Patricia Davids

Steeple
Hill®

Published by Steeple Hill Books™

Special thanks and acknowledgment to
Patricia Davids for her contribution to the
After the Storm miniseries.

STEEPLE HILL BOOKS

Steeple
Hill®

ISBN-13: 978-0-373-81438-1

A FAMILY FOR THANKSGIVING

Copyright © 2009 by Harlequin Books S.A.

Printed in U.S.A.

Cast your cares on the Lord,
and he will sustain you;
he will never let the righteous fall.
—*Psalms* 55:22

This book is dedicated with respect and deep admiration to the people of Chapman, Kansas. Go Irish!

Prologue

～

July 10, 4:04 p.m.

"It's only a thunderstorm. It'll be over soon."

Huddled in the basement of the High Plains Community Church with her preschool class and numerous townspeople, Nicki Appleton tried to maintain a brave front for her kids. The howling wind sounded as if it were trying to rip the building apart. The old wooden structure shuddered and groaned over their heads in protest.

The lights flickered. Some of the children around her whimpered with fear.

"Don't be scared." One of Nicki's students, three-year-old Layla Logan, was patting the shoulder of a little girl sitting beside her.

Nicki couldn't help but smile at the child's motherly

tone. Maya Logan would be proud of her brave little daughter.

Glancing at the small basement window near the top of the wall, all Nicki could see were the limbs of the nearby cedar trees thrashing wildly and the greenish-gray sky beyond. A flash followed by a deafening clap of thunder made her jump.

Suddenly, hail began pelting the roof and bouncing off the ground outside the window. In a matter of seconds, marble-size chunks of ice were filling the window well.

Even by Kansas standards, this was a wicked storm.

At least her car wasn't getting hammered in the parking lot outside. Nicki breathed a quick prayer of thanks that she had chosen to walk to work leaving her car safely under the carport at her apartment.

Then abruptly, the wind and hail stopped. Nicki tensed. Something wasn't right.

The thought had barely formed in her mind when a great roar began. Like a dozen jet engines bearing down on them, the sound filled the church basement, drowning out the frightened cries of the people sheltering there.

Tornado!

Nicki pulled the youngest children closer to her, sheltering them with her body. Her ears popped in the intense pressure change. Dust filled the air. The lights went out. People screamed.

The roar went on and on until Nicki thought she would scream, too. It seemed like forever but, in reality, it only lasted a few minutes. Finally, the noise died away, and the sounds of the children's crying rose in volume.

"I'm scared."

"Turn on the lights, Miss Appleton."

"It's okay." Nicki used her calm teacher voice, although she felt anything but. Her heart was hammering hard enough to jump out of her body.

Close by in the darkness, Josie Cane added her reassurances to her daycare group. "It's fine. Everyone sit quietly, please."

Nicki fumbled, with shaking hands, for the flashlight in her emergency kit. Locating the plastic cylinder, she snapped it on.

The sudden bright circle of light showed her a dozen frightened, tear-streaked faces looking to her guidance. A sweep around the room revealed neighbors and friends taking stock of themselves and each other. Josie had her arms around her eight-year-old niece, Alyssa, planting a kiss on the girl's cheek.

Everyone seemed okay.

Thank You, dear Lord.

Nicki forced herself to smile at her class. "Wow! That was scary, wasn't it? Is everyone all right?"

Most of the children nodded. Layla, her brown eyes wide with fright, had her arms clasped around her crying friend. The Baker twins were still covering their ears with their hands. Together, they sobbed, "I want Mommy. I wanna go home."

Josie's flashlight snapped on next. She said, "We need to stay here a little longer."

The two women exchanged knowing glances. They didn't dare lead the children upstairs until they were sure it was safe. Nicki had no idea what awaited them.

The church's minister, Michael Garrison, quickly assumed charge. "Everyone stay put until we check things out."

He headed for the stairs followed by two other men. After several long, tense minutes, Michael returned and approached Nicki and Josie. His face registered such shock that Nicki bit her lower lip in trepidation. "How bad is it?"

"Really bad. The town took a direct hit, but at least the church and school building are intact."

Nicki stood on trembling legs. "Do you think it's safe to take the kids to their classroom? I think they'll be more comfortable in familiar surroundings."

"That's a good idea. We'll need this space to set up an emergency shelter."

"Why not use the carriage house?" she asked, knowing the building behind the church had been converted into a family shelter for emergencies several years ago.

"It's gone. Completely destroyed."

Her mouth fell open in shock. "But it's only a dozen yards from here."

"We were spared by the grace of God. There's no doubt about that."

Pressing a hand to her forehead, she started to turn away, but he grasped her arm. "Nicki, I know you must be worried about your home and your mother, but I need you to stay with the children—I don't know for how long."

Understanding all that he didn't say, she nodded. "My mother is out of town, thank Heaven. I'll stay as long as any of the kids need me."

Once upstairs, Nicki and Josie struggled to keep the scared children calm in the preschool room until their parents came for them. Nicki's friend, Maya Logan, was among the first to arrive. She snatched up Layla and covered her face with kisses.

Although Nicki was happy to see Maya was safe, the damage she described made Nicki sick to her stomach. It seemed that much of the downtown was in ruins.

With each new arrival, Nicki learned more about the destruction. Nearly half of High Plains had sustained serious damage. Power lines were down, even the cell-phone towers were off-line. Many streets were blocked by debris, including the bridge over the river, the main highway into town. Rescue teams had to travel miles out of their way to reach the stricken area.

The one bright note she heard was that the area of town where she lived had been spared.

Nearly two hours after the tornado struck, Reverend Michael found time to check on Nicki and her charges. Noting his disheveled appearance as he entered the preschool room, she asked, "How's it going?"

"Outside help is beginning to arrive. We've got a medical triage tent set up on the lawn. There are a lot of injuries."

"Any fatalities?" she asked softly, not wanting the children to overhear.

"Not so far, but some of the town and outlying areas haven't been searched. Apparently, there was more than one twister in this storm."

"Have you seen Josie? Alyssa and her little friend, Lily Marstow, slipped away from us. Josie went to look for them."

"I saw them all with Silas Marstow a few minutes ago."

"Oh, good." Nicki sagged with relief, happy to know her friend and the children were okay. Lily's father, Silas, was the only parent that hadn't been accounted for. She crossed his name off the list she'd made.

Michael looked at the half-dozen children playing around the room. "I see you still have a few kids left."

"Some people opted to leave their little ones here knowing they're in a safe place. They've gone out to help family and friends. I don't mind watching the children. I'm happy to help any way I can."

"What you're doing is deeply appreciated."

Nicki nodded toward four children playing with hand puppets in the corner. "The Jensen girls and the Baker twins don't have homes left. Their parents are trying to make arrangements of some kind for tonight."

"I'll speak to them. We still have a few empty cots in the basement. Shall I send Avery in to give you a hand?"

Nicki shook her head, declining the help of his fourteen-year-old niece. "I'm fine, but thanks for the offer."

"Okay, I'll put her to work elsewhere. I'd better get back. There is so much to do...." His weary voice trailed away as he walked out.

It was another hour before the last of her students had been handed over to family members. When they were all gone, Nicki walked outside the church with trepidation.

She had been right to be scared. She barely recognized the town she'd lived in all her life. Shredded insulation hung like tattered pink flags from the remains of broken, leafless trees. Whole houses were simply missing. Unrecognizable twisted pieces of metal, broken lumber and fallen masonry blocked much of Main Street. People were wandering around in a state of shock.

A TV news crew from a nearby city had set up beside a mobile van and were interviewing survivors and filming the wreckage. Help in the form of firefighters, ambulances and heavy equipment had begun pouring in. The sounds of sirens filled the evening air.

Walking toward the park, Nicki saw that the Old Town Hall had been reduced to a pile of rubble. It broke her heart to see the historic site in ruins, but it wasn't until she saw the leveled gazebo in the center of the park that tears filled her eyes and slid down her cheeks.

Her special place was gone.

An elderly woman, looking lost and confused, stopped beside Nicki. Grasping a broken umbrella in one hand and a battered fedora in the other, the woman said, "I can't find my husband. Frank never goes out without his hat."

Nicki put her own pain aside when she saw the woman was bleeding from a deep gash on her forearm. Ignoring the newsman that had run over to snap their picture, Nicki gently said, "I'll help you find him, but let's get you fixed up first."

"I don't know where he could have gone."

Taking the woman's elbow, Nicki led her back to the church grounds where the triage tent had been erected on the lawn. As Nicki turned her charge over to a paramedic at the scene, a tall gray-haired man with a bandage on his forehead rushed forward and engulfed the woman in a fierce hug.

Nicki swallowed around the lump in her throat.

Thank You, Lord, for this one happy ending. Please let there be many more.

Stepping out of the tent, Nicki saw a group of women manning tables of food and drinks for the rescue workers and residents. When one waved her over, Nicki gladly joined them. She simply couldn't go home. Not when there was so much to be done.

Many long hours later, a bleary-eyed Reverend Garrison accepted a sandwich from her and said, "It's after four o'clock in the morning, Nicki. You should go home. There'll be plenty of work left to do tomorrow."

Wearily, she nodded. "You're right."

"I'll get one of the police to take you."

"They have enough to do. It's only a short walk."

He started to argue, but someone called him away for yet another emergency.

Nicki left the churchyard and trudged toward her duplex with exhaustion pulling at every fiber in her body. She was only halfway home when her flashlight blinked out.

"Oh, not now!" She banged it against her palm, but it stubbornly remained dark. Like her town, or what was left of her town. She couldn't remember ever seeing the city without a single light glowing anywhere.

When her eyes had adjusted to the darkness, she realized the three-quarter moon in the sky offered just enough illumination to let her navigate. She started walking again, skirting the downed limbs and debris that littered the roadway.

The sounds of sirens and chain saws had finally begun to lessen. The prevailing odor of diesel fumes was beginning to dissipate, leaving only the smells of wet wood, churned dirt and mangled cedars to tint the muggy night air.

When she finally reached her apartment, she stopped and stared in disbelief. The tall maple tree in her front yard was lying uprooted as if pushed over by a giant hand. Its gnarled roots fanned into the air like a grotesque skirt. Part of its branches rested on her half of the duplex's roof.

She glanced at her neighbor's dark front window. She knew Lori Martin, a nurse at a hospital in nearby Manhattan, had gone to work the previous morning. Given the number of injuries that had been transported to the bigger medical center and the state of the roads, Nicki wondered if Lori had made it home.

Nicki decided against knocking to check. If her neighbor had gotten back into town, there was no sense waking her up at this hour to point out a fallen tree that Lori would have seen for herself.

Bracing herself to discover the worst inside her own place, Nicki walked around the gaping hole in the lawn and up her steps. Inside the house, it was so dark she couldn't see her hand in front of her face. Was that a blessing?

After locating spare batteries in a drawer in the kitchen, she managed to replace the ones in her flashlight. Holding her breath, she clicked the button.

The burst of light showed a room that looked exactly as she'd left it the previous morning when she hurried out the door to her preschool class. The sight was so welcome that tears stung her eyes.

Making her way through her small apartment, she found the living room and bathroom were also intact. Opening the door to her bedroom, she discovered she hadn't completely escaped the storm's wrath. A tree limb jutted through her window.

The branch had knocked everything off the top of her dresser. Cherished mementos, photos and odds and ends were broken and scattered about. The carpet was wet from the rain that had blown in. Wearily she gathered up her smashed treasures and placed them on her bedside stand. Those that couldn't be salvaged she threw into the trash can along with the broken shards of window glass.

Straightening, her flashlight caught the reflection of something bright behind the leaves on the dresser top. She stepped closer and saw it was a silver heart-shaped frame—the one photo she should have tossed out years ago.

Picking it up, she turned it over surprised to find the glass intact and the picture undamaged. It was her senior-prom photo. Nicki sat on her bed and stared at the couple in the snapshot. Had she really been that young, that carefree?

The strapless blue dress and upswept hairdo were meant to make a giggling teenager look mature. In retrospect she looked silly, but Clay Logan, Maya's brother, in his cowboy hat and Western suit looked incredibly handsome. His deep blue eyes surveyed the world as if he owned it all, including her heart.

Before now, all that remained of that magical high school night was this photo and the old gazebo in the park—the place where they'd shared their first kiss and experienced the giddy rush of teenage hormones. Even though she was the one who'd called a halt to their passion before it went too far, she believed that Clay understood and respected her. She knew in her heart that their kiss was the beginning of something special between them.

Her girlish, romantic illusions came to an abrupt end the following day, when she learned Clay had left town without a word to her.

To say she had been crushed was an understatement. More than anything, she had considered Clay her friend.

"Friends don't run out on friends without saying goodbye," she muttered.

But he had gone. Now, the old gazebo was gone, too. Blown to bits by the vicious wind.

Snapping off the light, Nicki pressed the cold metal picture frame to her chest. She was too weary to face an old heartbreak.

Yet maybe this *was* the time to face it. To let go of the last bit of hope that wouldn't die. She was a practical, twenty-five-year-old woman not a naive eighteen-year-old kid. Clay wasn't coming back.

Turning the frame over again, she removed the backing. A postcard fell into her lap. She didn't need the flashlight to read it, she knew it by heart. The postmark said Amarillo, there was only one line written in Clay's bold hand: *You're better off without me.*

He was so right. She *was* better off without a man who broke her heart to go wandering the country.

Nicki turned her flashlight back on and stared at the picture in her hand. Enough wallowing in the past. It was time to look to the future. There was a whole lot of rebuilding to be done.

Tossing the framed photo and postcard into the trash on top of the shattered window glass, Nicki lay down on her bed to grab a few hours of sleep.

She dreamed about the howling wind and Clay Logan's bright blue eyes.

For the next two days, Nicki was simply too busy helping with the cleanup of her town to think about the photo she'd thrown away. Her few broken treasures seemed trivial compared to the losses she saw around her. Dozens of her neighbors had lost everything. Sadly, Maya Logan's sister-in-law, Marie, had lost her life. Working side by side with volunteers who'd come from all over to help, Nicki gained a new appreciation for the kindness that strangers could bestow on those in need and for the resilient spirit of the people of High Plains.

The ring of her cell phone offered her a break from the hot, exhausting job of carrying tree limbs and broken boards to a waiting dump truck. Pulling off her gloves, she extracted the phone from her pocket. The phone company had gotten one of their towers back online the day after the storm, allowing for cellular service, but the city was still without land lines or electricity. She flipped open her cell and said, "Hello?"

"Nicki, I'm glad to hear your voice. Are you all right? This is just so terrible." It was Emma Barnet, a social worker Nicki knew well and had worked with on several occasions.

"I'm fine. I had one broken window. How about you?"

"It missed our house by a mile. I'm happy you're okay, because this is an official call. A toddler was brought into the hospital the night of the tornado. A little girl about fifteen months old. We haven't been able to locate her parents or any family. No one knows who she is. She was found by the old cottages near the river."

"No one has claimed a child? That's unbelievable!"

"The authorities are working on identifying her, but it may take a while since she isn't old enough to give us a name. I know this is an imposition at a time like this, but the hospital is over capacity. I'm swamped with people who need placement and every kind of help."

"Tell me what I can do."

Sighing, Emma said, "Bless you, Nicki. I don't want to send this little girl out of the area if I don't have to. Is there any way you can foster her until we find her family?"

Nicki didn't hesitate. "Of course."

"Great. Since you've fostered babies before, the paperwork will be minimal. We're calling her Kasey for now because she had the initials K.C. inside her shirt. She's got a nasty bump on her head plus scrapes and bruises, but nothing serious. We should be able to release her from the hospital in a day or two."

"Then I should start coming by to visit so she can get used to me before I take her home. I'll be there in a few hours."

"That sounds perfect. If anything changes, I'll call."

Snapping the phone shut, Nicki looked at the unbelievable devastation around her. Out of all this sorrow there had to come something good. Perhaps this unknown little girl would be it.

Chapter One

October 27

Clay Logan had barely stepped down from his horse before Mrs. Dewey threw her arms around him again.

"Thank you, Clay. Thank you so very, very much."

His neck was going to have a permanent crick in it if she didn't let up soon.

Her husband, standing beside the second trail horse, lifted his seven-year-old daughter, Karen, out of the saddle. Walking over, he grabbed Clay's hand in a vicelike grip and began pumping it up and down. "We owe you a debt of gratitude that we'll never be able to repay."

Clay's boss, Hollister Dodd, owner of the Canadian Wilderness Guide Service, had come out onto the wide porch of the lodge at the Chilihota Ranch. He watched the return of his clients from their packhorse excursion with a puzzled expression on his face.

"It was nothing, ma'am. Honest," Clay managed to mutter past Mrs. Dewey's stranglehold.

She took a step back. "I don't know how you can say that. You saved our daughter's life!"

"What's this?" Hollister came forward to take the reins of Mrs. Dewey's horse.

"Tanner pushed me in the lake." Safe in her father's arms, Karen, a blond-haired, blue-eyed pixie and the bane of Clay's existence for the last two weeks, scowled at her older brother still sitting on his horse.

"It was an accident," fourteen-year-old Tanner mumbled.

Something in his tone caught Clay's attention and brought back memories of his own childhood. His brother, Jesse, used to sound just like that when he was explaining why Clay had landed in trouble while Jesse was supposed to be watching him.

Hollister's gaze focused on Clay. "When did this happen?"

Mr. Dewey spoke up quickly. "Please don't think Clay was negligent in any way. We made camp last evening at White Lake. The kids were horsing around on that big boulder that juts out like a ship's prow. Clay cautioned them several times to get off the rock."

He had, but little miss daredevil just had to see

how close to the edge she could get. In a way, she reminded Clay of himself at that age. No wonder Jesse had been glad to see the last of him.

Hollister relaxed once he realized the family didn't intend to sue him for all he was worth. Stepping up to Mr. Dewey, he ruffled Karen's hair. "I'll bet it was a cold dip."

She nodded, and Clay had to agree. His dive from the rock ledge fifteen feet up had plunged him deep into the frigid waters of the snow-fed lake. The shock all but paralyzed his muscles. Even now, he marveled that he'd managed to reach the girl in the icy depths and find the strength to get them both to shore.

Mrs. Dewey pressed her hand to her heart as tears welled up in her eyes. "When Karen fell, Clay didn't hesitate. He jumped in to save her. I don't know what would have happened if he hadn't acted so quickly." Her voice cracked, and she couldn't go on.

Her husband reached out to draw her close. She buried her face in his shoulder, her arms encircling both her husband and her child. Mr. Dewey said, "Karen can't swim. Clay saved her life."

In spite of their praise, Clay knew he hadn't done it alone.

Even now, he wasn't sure he trusted what he'd felt, but it had been as real as the icy water around him. Deep beneath the surface, at the moment all his energy had been sapped and he was sure Karen was lost forever, a healing presence had come over him. It gave him the strength he needed to reach the child and get her to shore.

God had been with him in that lake. He had no other explanation.

After the death of his parents when he was nineteen, Clay felt God had abandoned him and his family. It seemed better to live life without trusting in an almighty power that had failed him so completely. Clay had turned his back on the faith he'd grown up with. To his way of thinking, God didn't care much about Clay Logan, so Clay Logan wouldn't care about Him.

It was something of a shock to discover he'd been wrong.

Mr. Dewey extended his hand to Clay again. "If there is ever anything I can do for you, young man, all you have to do is ask."

Looking stunned at the tale, Hollister asked, "Does Karen need to see a doctor? I'll be happy to cover the cost."

Karen scowled fiercely at him. "No! I won't go to the doctor, and you can't make me. He'll give me shots."

Mrs. Dewey wiped the tears from her cheeks with her palms. "You don't have to have any shots, honey."

Mr. Dewey shrugged. "It's amazing, but she seems fine."

"I'd feel better if you at least spoke to a doctor about this. Come inside and use my phone."

With Hollister leading the way, the trio followed him into the lodge leaving Tanner still sitting on his horse.

Clay studied the boy's dejected posture. He knew something of what the boy had to be feeling. "Care to give me a hand putting the horses away?"

"I guess."

Dismounting, Tanner fell into step beside Clay as they led the animals to the barn. Inside, the building held a dozen large stalls filled with thick straw waiting to give the weary trail ponies a well-deserved rest. The warm smell of horses, grain and hay were scents Clay knew well. He'd grown up on a ranch, and he'd spent his whole life as a cowboy.

Side by side, Clay and Tanner worked in silence following the routine Clay had taught the teen and his family during their trek into the wilderness. The boy's attention to detail, his willingness to follow directions and lend a hand had made him an ideal partner on their recent trip, unlike his less-than-helpful little sister.

"I didn't push her. I was trying to pull her back from the edge," Tanner said at last, as he slowly brushed down his mare.

"I'm not sure I'd blame you if you had. I considered it more than once." Clay pulled the heavy saddle and sweaty blanket off his horse and threw it over the stall door with ease.

Chuckling, Tanner began brushing with renewed vigor. "She is a pain."

"No kidding. You have my sympathy."

"Mom and my stepdad spoil her rotten."

"And anything she does wrong you get blamed for because you're the oldest."

Tanner looked surprised. "You must have a sister, too."

"I do. Her name is Maya, but she wasn't the one who caused the trouble in our family. That was all me."

"Is your sister the oldest?"

"No, she's the baby, but I have an older brother."

Neither of which he'd seen in seven years. Had it really been that long? How much longer would it be until Jesse forgave him? Would he ever?

And what about Nicki? Did she ever think about him? He thought about her far too often.

Each time Clay received a call from Maya he wanted to ask about Nicki, but jumping off a fifteen-foot cliff into a freezing lake was a whole lot easier.

"How can I get a job like this?" Tanner asked, breaking into Clay's somber thoughts.

"You bum around for a while, take odd jobs on ranches, wander farther and farther away." His voice trailed off as the aimlessness of his past hit him.

Was that all his life had been up to this point? Where did it go from here?

"Away from what?" Tanner asked.

"For me, a place called High Plains, Kansas."

Away from the windswept prairie. From the rolling Flint Hills covered in deep green grass where cattle grew fat and sleek and a boy could ride all day without seeing anyone but a lone hawk circling overhead against a sky so blue it hurt his eyes.

Clay patted his horse's neck as he stared at the snowcapped Rocky Mountains outside the doorway without really seeing them. Instead, he saw Nicki looking shy and beautiful; saw the moonlight reflected in her eyes as she gazed up at him inside the gazebo by the river.

He'd kissed a few women since that night, but none of them matched the sweetness of Nicki's lips.

And all he'd done for her in return was to sully her good name.

He could still hear Jesse's voice raised in anger condemning Clay for ruining her reputation and for so much more unspoken between them. A condemnation Clay knew he deserved.

He glanced at Tanner. The boy was still waiting for his advice. "Ask Mr. Dodd about hiring you on as a summer hand. If he and your folks say yes, then prove you're reliable and willing to do the tough jobs. After a year or two of learning the ropes he might let you guide."

"My stepdad wants me to start working for him when I turn sixteen, but I'd rather be a cowboy."

Clay threw back his head and laughed. "Your dad owns the largest hotel-building company in Dallas. He's worth millions of dollars. Go to work for him. It'll pay a whole lot better."

Tanner managed a sheepish grin. "Will you be here next year?"

"Will your folks leave the princess back at the castle?"

"Not much chance of that."

"Then I may be looking for work elsewhere. Two weeks with that girl's fits and tantrums was more than enough for me."

This had been his last trip of the season. Soon, the mountains and valleys would be covered in a snow blanket that would last until April. Hollister had already offered to let Clay stay on over the winter, but he hadn't made up his mind yet. He'd been guiding here for three years, the longest he'd spent in one place since leaving home, but lately he'd been feeling restless again. Like it was time to move on.

"Do you have kids?" Tanner asked.

"Me?" Clay shook his head. "I'm not the settle-down-raise-a-family kind of guy. That's my brother's thing."

Why was it that his words didn't carry the conviction he normally felt? Maybe it was because Tanner reminded him so much of Jesse, and Jesse had been on Clay's mind a lot.

He should have been there for Jesse when his wife died.

Clay moved to the second horse waiting to be unsaddled. He hadn't learned about Marie's death until three weeks after the fact. The phone call from Maya back in July had missed Clay by two days. By then, he'd been deep in the Canadian wilderness with a hunting party and couldn't be reached.

He returned his sister's call as soon as he got back to the lodge, but her home and cell phones had both been disconnected. Worried sick, he'd gritted his teeth and called Jesse to find out what was going on.

It was the first time the brothers had spoken in seven years.

Clay could still hear the hard, stilted tone of Jesse's voice as he recounted how his wife had been killed during a tornado that touched down in the area.

Thousands of miles away and weeks after her death, Clay hadn't known what to say. His heart went out to Jesse, but he couldn't find the words he needed to offer his brother comfort. It had always been that way between them. How could two sons of the same parents be so different?

Clay had finally asked, "Do you want me to come home?"

Oh, how he needed Jesse to say yes, but his tough-as-nails sibling replied, "Don't rush back on my account. We've managed without you this long."

It didn't take a genius to read between the lines. What Jesse meant was don't come back at all. Jesse hadn't forgiven Clay for his role in the death of their parents. The hurt went bone-deep.

Clay had gone back into the wilderness with his next group of clients a few days later. Weeks after his call to Jesse, Clay learned about his sister's marriage in much the same fashion. This time, there had been a letter waiting for him when he got back to the ranch.

He would have liked to have been there for Maya's big day, but it seemed that she and her new husband, Greg Garrison, were in a hurry so they could foster a six-year-old boy named Tommy Jacobs.

Since Maya already had a three-year-old daughter, Clay realized he now had more relatives that he hadn't met than ones he knew. Jesse had triplet daughters that were only a few months old, and he was raising them by himself. Jesse never did things the easy way.

"High Plains, Kansas. Where is that?" Tanner asked. "My grandparents live in Wichita."

From behind them, Karen's know-it-all voice cut

in. "That's where my class sent a big card on the first day of school. We all signed it."

"Oh, right," Tanner replied. "The town that was almost wiped out by a tornado."

Clay glanced between the kids. "Are you sure you aren't thinking of Greensburg?"

Karen's face scrunched into a scowl. She threw a handful of straw at Clay. "My teacher said High Plains!"

"Karen, be nice," Tanner chided.

"You're not the boss of me," she shot back, making a face and sticking her tongue out at him.

Tanner finished his horse and turned the animal loose in the stall. "She's right. It was High Plains. It was all over the news for a couple of days. If Mr. Hollister will let us use his computer, I can show you the story on the Internet."

Karen rolled her eyes. "We could have used mine, but Dad wouldn't let me bring my laptop. He said this was going to be a real old-fashioned vacation."

Clay gaped at her. "You have a laptop? Aren't you in, what, the first grade?"

She snatched up two more handfuls of straw to fling at him. "Second grade!"

Karen's brush with death hadn't reduced her sassiness one bit.

Tanner walked toward the barn door. "Ignore her. It works for me."

Fifteen minutes later, Clay was leaning over Tanner's shoulder as he pulled up picture after picture of High Plains, shredded by a tornado. Hundred-year-old trees stripped bare, building and cars reduced to shattered jumbles of rubble.

Why hadn't Jesse or Maya told him about this? *Because they think I don't care.*

Maya had mentioned in her letter that the cleanup was continuing after the storm and that she and Greg were planning to hold a wedding reception in the Old Town Hall when repairs were finished, hopefully by Christmas. She'd also written to expect an invitation.

Clay had no idea the damage to High Plains had been so severe. He couldn't believe he had to find out what had happened to his hometown from strangers when he'd spoken to Jesse on the phone only weeks after the event.

Clay had to acknowledge that he hadn't exactly stayed on the line to chitchat with Jesse after learning about Marie's death. Had Maya assumed Jesse filled Clay in on the details of the storm? She must have, or she would have tried contacting him again.

With a sinking heart, he realized his silence all these months probably convinced her he *didn't* care.

Next, Tanner brought up a national news story about the storm's aftermath. As shots of the devastation flashed by in a slide show, Clay stared at them in shock. He recognized the ruins as buildings in the downtown area. The town he knew was all but gone. Wiped out in a day.

Suddenly, a familiar face flashed onto the screen. A second later another picture of a broken building replaced it.

Clay gripped Tanner's shoulder. "Stop. Go back."

Tanner did as he asked. Clay leaned closer to the monitor. Nicki stood in front of a pile of rubble with her arm around an old woman clinging to a broken umbrella. Nicki's face glistened with tears.

His heart ached for the look of loss in her eyes, but she was still the most beautiful woman he'd ever seen. Time hadn't changed that.

He read the caption under the photo: "High Plains residents console each other near the ruins of their historic Old Town Hall."

Clay closed his eyes as a feeling of helplessness swallowed him whole. He should be there. Jesse, Maya, Nicki, the whole community had suffered a terrible loss, and he hadn't done a thing to help.

"Is that someone you know?" Tanner's voice broke into Clay's thoughts.

"Yeah." Someone he used to know. Someone he'd left behind a long time ago. What a stupid, stupid mistake that had been.

Shame, anger and guilt had driven Clay out of

town. His juvenile pride had kept him away. All this time. All this wasted time.

The next page Tanner brought up was dated the previous month. It was a story about the rebuilding efforts in High Plains. According to the article, the first overwhelming response of volunteers had dwindled leaving much of the town still struggling to recover.

With startling clarity Clay saw what he needed to do, saw for the first time in his life the path God wanted him to follow.

He patted Tanner's shoulder. "Thanks for showing me this."

Turing around, Clay strode out of the inner office and crossed the lobby to where his boss stood beside the wide stone fireplace visiting with Mr. and Mrs. Dewey.

"Hollister, I'm leaving. Send my last paycheck to my sister. You've got her address."

The man's craggy features settled into a scowl. "Leaving? Where're you going?"

Clay was already halfway out the door. He paused and looked over his shoulder. "Somewhere I should have gone a long time ago. Home."

One second Nicki was walking down the sidewalk across from the construction site at the Old Town Hall and the next second her world tipped sideways.

Stumbling to a halt, she blinked and looked again. The mirage didn't vanish. The heavy thud of her heart stole her breath, leaving her numb with shock.

Clay Logan stood not fifty feet away, his hands shoved in the pockets of a brown sheepskin-lined jacket as he hunched against the cutting wind. It was only the second day of November, but the deep chill in the air was a reminder that winter wasn't far away.

What was Clay doing here? How long had he been back in town? How long was he staying?

He hadn't seen her. She was thankful for that small favor as she struggled to regain her composure. He was surveying a bare patch of earth ringed with old concrete footings. It was all that remained of the large gazebo that once stood in the middle of the town's park.

Was he as saddened by its loss as she had been?

So much of the tornado-ravaged town was in the process of being rebuilt, homes, businesses, the historic Old Town Hall. Fixing the gazebo wasn't even on the list of things the overwhelmed city council had planned.

Besides, another gazebo would never be the same.

As if aware that someone was watching him, Clay turned to look in her direction. His shoulders stiffened. For a long instant they stared at each other without moving. Then, he touched the brim of his black cowboy hat to acknowledge her.

She wished she were closer, wished she could see the expression in his eyes.

Was the love still there?

Of course it wasn't. What a foolish thing to wonder. They'd been starry-eyed teenagers the last time they'd seen each other.

Don't just stand here. Walk away. Pretend it doesn't matter that he's back, she told herself.

She wouldn't let it matter. She'd wasted enough years of her life hoping for his return. Forcing herself to take a step, she flinched when she realized he was already moving toward her, closing the distance.

Turning around and running in the opposite direction suddenly seemed like a good idea. But running away was Clay's specialty, not hers.

The thought stiffened her spine. She shifted her large green-and-orange striped tote to her other shoulder and waited. As he approached, she saw that the years had changed his good looks from boyish charm into chiseled masculinity.

Dark stubble covered his square chin and the planes of his cheeks. Crow's-feet at the corners of his deep blue eyes added character to his face, but the soft grin that pulled at one corner of his mouth was still the same one she remembered.

A swirl of butterflies filled her midsection. The sight of that slow smile aimed in her direction used to melt her heart like butter in a hot pan.

Stop. What am I doing?

Nicki gathered her scattered wits. Roguish grin or not, she wasn't about to fall back into some bygone, teenage hero-worship mode. She had far too much sense for that.

Time to start acting like it.

"As I live and breathe, if it isn't Clay Logan. I almost didn't recognize you. What's it been, five years?" She was proud that her tone carried just the right touch of indifference. If only he didn't notice the white-knuckled grip she had on the strap of her bag.

His smile disappeared. "It's been seven years, Nicki."

"That long?" She tsked as she shook her head. "Time sure flies, doesn't it?"

She swept one hand toward the park indicating the broken trees and rubble piles that hadn't yet been removed. "As you can see, things have changed a lot since you were here."

"I guess they have," he replied, a sad quality in his voice. His gaze never left her.

Tipping her head to one side, she narrowed her eyes. "You didn't really expect things would be the same as when you left, did you?"

He pulled off his hat and ran his fingers through his dark hair. "No, but I wasn't prepared for exactly how different things would be."

At that moment, he looked lost and uncertain.

Sympathy overrode her ire. She'd had four months to become accustomed to the scarred face of High Plains. He must be seeing it for the first time. It had to be painful.

She said, "The tornado really made a mess of things. The downtown area was hit pretty hard. The General Store is gone, as are most of the homes south of Garrison Street between First and Second."

Still holding his hat, he used it to point toward the line of broken trees in the park that ran between the High Plains river and the town's Main Street. "It's hard to believe only one person was killed."

"Yes. God was with us. The carriage house beside the church and the Old Town Hall both took direct hits. Volunteers from the community are rebuilding the hall, as you can see. The hope is that it'll be done in time to hold the Founders' Day celebration on Christmas Day."

"Looks like they're making good progress."

"With the outside, yes, but the inside is still bare studs."

"What about you? Did you lose much?"

Waving a hand to dismiss her minor losses, she said, "A broken window. That was all." And the photo of the two of them that she'd tossed in the trash that night.

Hitching her bag higher, she flashed a bright

smile. "I need to get going. It was good seeing you again, Clay."

Stepping around him, she was surprised when he reached out and took hold of her elbow. "Nicki, I'm sorry."

Don't do this, Clay. Not after all this time. I waited so long for you.

Keeping the smile on her face cost her dearly. Her cheek muscles ached with the effort. "What are you sorry about?"

He studied her with a puzzled frown. "For taking off like that."

Was he really expecting her to just forgive him? To say the last seven years didn't matter? She had *some* pride. There was no way she'd let him see how much he'd hurt her.

"It's water under the bridge, Clay. We were just kids. It wasn't like we were soul mates or something."

He didn't reply, but he released her. His hand dropped to his side. "I'm glad you didn't hold it against me."

Her mind screamed at her to leave before he saw though the veil she'd pulled over her turbulent emotions, but she couldn't stop drinking in the sight of him. The urge to fling herself into his arms and hug him was overwhelming. Why did he still have such an effect on her?

Forcing herself to take a step back, she quickly

said, "I hope you enjoy your visit. I know Maya and Jesse must be excited that you're home."

A hint of his grin reappeared as he settled his Stetson on his head. "Maya might be happy. Jesse? I'm thinking not so much."

Chapter Two

Clay called himself every kind of fool in the book as he faced Nicki. He'd spent the last seven years wondering if she'd forgiven him for running out on her.

Turns out, she'd barely given it a thought.

She was the reason he'd come back. Her picture, the one of her with tears in her eyes, had solidified a yearning he'd never truly understood. His heart ached at the sight of her while she acted as if it meant nothing—as if there'd never been anything between them.

Maybe there hadn't been. Maybe his imagination had taken a simple high school infatuation and worked it into something special because he thought he'd never see her again.

During the past five days on the road south, he'd had plenty of time to think about what he was doing, but it wasn't until he rolled into town that he began to question the wisdom of leaving a job and coming back to an uncertain welcome.

Was this really the path God wanted him to take?

Faith, the idea of trusting God to guide him, was too new. He'd been a loner for years, trusting only himself, trying not to care too much about anyone or anything. Until now.

Raking a hand through her curly blond hair, Nicki took a step back as if she intended to walk away, but she didn't. Instead, she said, "If you're worried about Jesse's reaction, I assume that means the two of you haven't reconciled."

It was the look of compassion in her eyes and the tone of her voice more than her words that gave him a sliver of hope. She remembered.

Nicki had been his sounding board during his last year of high school. She knew that he and his brother didn't see eye to eye on anything. She'd been a good friend. He let her down—the way he'd let everyone down.

"I'm not sure Jesse and I'll ever reconcile. He blames me for Mom and Dad's death."

"Not as much as you blame yourself."

She'd always been good at reading him. Clay swallowed hard as old emotions threatened to swamp him. It *had* been his fault. Nothing would change that fact.

"You can shop all day for another guilty party, but

you won't find one. It was my idea to climb up and spray-paint graffiti on the Alma water tower that night, a stupid, dangerous stunt if there ever was one. I was the one who got arrested. I was one who called Dad to come bail me out."

He swallowed hard against the pain of those memories. "If I hadn't done it, Dad and Mom wouldn't have been in the car when that semi crossed the center line. We'd still have parents, and Jesse and Maya wouldn't hate my guts."

"They don't hate you, Clay. You're their brother."

"Okay, maybe Maya doesn't, she always was the peace-keeper in the family. But Jesse hates me."

"I'm sure you're mistaken."

"I've talked to him on the phone once since I left. He told me his wife had been killed, then he told me not to come home. It was pretty clear. I'm not welcome."

She looked down, as if at a loss for words. Clay studied her face. He'd dreamed of her so often that he thought he knew her every feature by heart. He remembered the face of a girl. The woman standing in front of him had a quiet strength about her that was new. She'd matured, grown more beautiful—if that was possible.

The blustery wind put color in her cheeks. A cluster of curls from her shoulder-length hair blew across her full lips. She used one hand to drag her hair back and tuck it behind her ear. It was a gesture she used to use just before she gave him one of her shy, sweet smiles. Seeing it brought a flood of memories.

The two of them studying before the big algebra test, finding the courage to ask her to the dance, walking with her in the moonlight.

Now that he was with her again he knew those memories would never be enough. He wanted new ones. He wanted to get to know this new woman all over again.

When she looked up he saw deep indecision written clearly on her features. "I really do need to get going, Clay."

He didn't want to see her go, but didn't know how to stop her from leaving. The irony of it wasn't lost on him. He was good at leaving, not at staying.

God, I believe You brought me home for a reason. Show me what it is.

He nodded and smiled politely. "Maybe I'll see you around."

He'd make sure of it.

A ghost of a smile curled the corner of her lips. "It's a small town."

"Smaller than it used to be."

She rolled her eyes. "That's the sad truth."

Sorry for his insensitive remark, he quickly added, "The people here know how to survive. My granddad told me the place was nearly wiped off the map just a few years after it was founded."

"Yes. I know the story. It's been repeated a lot lately."

He followed her gaze across the road to where the shell of the rebuilt Old Town Hall stood out like a sore thumb, all glaring new plywood and silver sheets of insulation. It was clear the town had copied the size and style of the old structure.

Glancing westward, he saw the church had survived intact. The sturdy, square white building was another relic of High Plains history. Its row of arched windows had looked upon the town's growth from a simple frontier mill town to a bustling city of more than three thousand residents.

Clay said, "I understand their need to replace that special part of their heritage."

"*Our* heritage," she said quietly. "It's your home, too."

His eyes locked with hers. Time stood still. It would only be home if he could find a way to earn back her friendship and her trust along with that of his brother and sister.

From down the street, someone called Nicki's name breaking the connection between them. He looked over her shoulder to see her mother coming toward them. Glenis Appleton was pushing a dark blue stroller with a bright-eyed toddler in it. Since the tyke looked like it had been swallowed alive by a hooded pink coat, Clay assumed it was a little girl.

Slightly breathless, Glenis stopped beside Nicki. "We finished early so we thought we'd met you halfway."

Stooping to the child's level, Nicki asked, "Did you have fun at Nana's quilting class?"

The little girl kicked her feet and jabbered with excitement.

Grinning, Glenis said, "She slept through the whole thing."

Nicki rose. "Thanks for taking her this afternoon. Mom, you remember Clay Logan, don't you?"

To say Nicki's mother looked stunned was putting it mildly.

Clay raised two fingers to touch the brim of his hat. "It's a pleasure to see you again, Mrs. Appleton."

As Glenis glanced between Clay and Nicki, her expression hardened. "I didn't know you were back in town, Clay."

"I just got in."

"I see." Her gaze switched to Nicki. "You should get Kasey out of this cold wind."

"You're right." Nicki accepted the stroller handles from her mother.

Her daughter eyed Clay seriously for a few seconds, then her round little face broke into a wide grin. She raised her hand and wiggled her fingers. "Hi. Hi."

Squatting in front of child, Clay reached in and flicked her nose. "Hi, yourself, sugar face."

Nicki pulled the stroller back a pace. "Come on, honey, let's get you home. Clay, it was nice seeing you again. Have a good visit."

Clay rose slowly and stood on the sidewalk staring after them as they walked away. His hopes, like the gazebo where he'd once kissed Nicki, had been reduced to ruins in a matter of seconds.

She had a child. He was too late.

Over the years Clay had considered the possibility that Nicki would find someone else. Sometimes, he even hoped that she'd found someone to love her as she deserved to be loved. But to see it— to know for certain she loved another man—cut deeper than he had imagined possible.

Nicki had gone on with her life. He hadn't.

Racing to her rescue had seemed like a good idea five days ago. As it turned out, he was years too late. She didn't need rescuing. Even the town he wanted to help rebuild was well on the way to recovery. He'd driven thousands of miles to discover no one needed him.

He ran a hand over the stubble on his chin. So what now?

Leave again? And go where? He'd been north, south, east and west of Kansas. What good had it done him? He might pretend he was a carefree cowboy, but the specter of his failures followed him wherever he traveled.

He'd made so many mistakes. Each one led to another and another until it seemed like his whole life had been one long string of screwups. Just as Jesse had predicted.

Give me a clue here, God. What am I supposed to do?

Somehow, Clay knew he needed to start over, to find what had been missing in his life. As much as he'd wanted that to be Nicki, it wasn't going to happen.

The knowledge was more depressing than the ruins of the town.

Nicki stopped at her front steps and lifted Kasey out of her stroller. Her mother folded the carrier and followed Nicki into the house.

Sitting on the camel-colored sofa, Nicki divested Kasey of her plush coat and mittens and waited for her mother to make some comment about Clay. She didn't have long to wait.

"Nicki, did you know Clay was coming back to High Plains?"

"Nope. I was as surprised to see him as you were." Surprised, angry, confused, attracted.

"I thought perhaps that was why you wanted me to watch Kasey today."

"I told you I had an appointment to get my hair

cut today." Grabbing a strand, she waved it toward her mother. "See—no split ends."

"I'm sorry. I didn't mean to imply that you were lying."

"Could have fooled me." Nicki leaned forward to tug Kasey's green knit top down over her plump little belly. As far as Nicki was concerned, it was one of her foster daughter's cutest features. Of course, her wheat-blond hair, bright blue eyes, dimpled cheeks and pudgy fingers were all a close second.

Kasey patted her chest. "Chirt."

Nicki beamed. "That's right. That's your shirt. You're so smart."

"Owey." Kasey pointed to the pink scar on her forehead.

"Yes, that was your owey, but it's all better now." Nicki planted a kiss on the spot to prove it.

Kasey had been found the night of the tornado injured and alone. She remained the great mystery of the storm. No one knew who she was. It was as if she had literally been dropped out of the sky.

Extensive investigations by the local and state police and even the National Center for Missing and Exploited Children had come up empty in the search for her family or her identity, though some imposters had claimed she was their daughter.

At first Nicki had prayed daily that Kasey would be reunited with her mother or her father. Knowing that someone, somewhere must be frantic about the child had fueled those prayers.

Lately, however, those prayers had become harder and harder to voice. Her love for her foster daughter was growing by leaps and bounds. The idea of losing her had become almost unbearable.

Glenis sat on the sofa beside Nicki. "I just thought it was odd that you should run into Clay Logan the moment he set foot in town."

"The Lord moves in mysterious ways, Mom."

Affronted, Glenis folded her hands in her lap. "I hardly think you need to be flippant about it. I remember how you cried yourself to sleep for weeks after that boy left."

"It was a long time ago. We were kids. I got over it."

"You say that, but I'm not so sure."

"Surely you don't think I've carried a torch for him all this time?"

"Well, haven't you?"

"No. I've dated any number of men, a few seriously. But because I haven't met the right man is no reason to assume I'm still pining over Clay. Besides, my friends have snapped up all the good men around here."

The tornado might have wreaked havoc on the town, but the twister had certainly brought with it a dose of romance. Maya Logan had fallen for her boss, Greg Garrison, the most eligible bachelor in town. They had married in August. Then the two of them quickly added Tommy Jacobs, a six-year-old foster child to their family.

Reverend Michael Garrison had recently become engaged to Heather Waters, the founder of Helping Hands Christian Mission. Heather, originally from High Plains, had returned to help with the recovery efforts, and it looked like she would be staying for good.

Josie Cane, who ran the after-school day-care program at the church where Nicki taught preschool, was head over heels in love with Silas Marstow. And engaged—thanks to the matchmaking efforts of Josie's niece and Silas's daughter.

Even Lexi Harmon, the town's veterinarian and her ex-husband, Colt Ridgeway, the police chief, had rekindled their marriage and were back together—where Nicki always thought they belonged.

It warmed Nicki's heart to see so many people she cared about finding love in the face of the town's tragedy, but sometimes she felt the green imp of jealousy sitting on her shoulder. Why hadn't it happened for her?

And now Clay Logan had returned.

No, don't even go there!

Nicki scolded herself for the unbidden thought. She hadn't pined for him. She wasn't waiting for him to show up. She was living the life God meant for her to live. That life didn't include a cowboy with wanderlust in his veins.

"I want you to be happy," her mother continued. "I want you to find someone you can settle down with."

Leaning forward, Nicki ruffled the baby's hair. "I am happy. I have someone. I have Kasey."

"You know that's not what I mean."

Nicki sat back and met her mother's critical stare. "The settling down kind of men I've met want children."

She tried hard not to sound bitter, but she couldn't help it. "Since I can't have children, that's been something of a date killer when the subject comes up."

"I'm sure there's a man out there willing to adopt a child once you're married."

"I'll keep looking for him. In the mean time, thanks again for watching Kasey. Let me buy you lunch next week as payment."

Glenis rose and bent to place a kiss on Kasey's head. "I don't need payment to watch this little doll."

Nicki smiled. "She is that."

After gathering up her purse and slipping into her dark blue wool coat, Glenis headed to the door. Nicki followed her, leaving Kasey happily pulling a half-dozen toys from a large red plastic bin at the end of the sofa until she found her favorite stuffed animal. A small pink bear given to her in the hospital by Layla Logan.

In the entryway, Glenis paused. "Are you working at the Old Town Hall tonight?"

"Yes. What about you?"

"Not tonight, I have a meeting of the library committee."

Giving her mother a quick hug, Nicki said, "You don't need to worry about me. I'm doing fine. I love my job. I love the kids I work with. I have a great life."

Glenis returned the hug. "Worrying is a mother's job."

"Then at least take a vacation day. I'm not throwing myself at Clay Logan's feet simply because he's back for a visit."

Glenis pulled open the door letting in a gust of cold wind. "I'm sorry if I upset you by talking about him."

"You didn't upset me," Nicki answered truthfully. Clay had done that without any help.

Where was he now? Had he gone out to the ranch? How long was he staying? Would she see him again?

Nicki crossed her arms against the chill as she closed the door behind her mother. All questions and no answers, that certainly summed up her relationship with Clay in the past.

Theirs had been a friendship she valued deeply. If only they had kept things friendly and not let their teenage emotions take over. What she felt back then hadn't been love. It had been a high school crush and nothing more.

In a way, it had been good for her to see Clay again. Perhaps now she truly could get over him the way she always claimed she had.

Chapter Three

Clay pulled his truck to a stop at the curb and checked the house numbers against the return address on his sister's last letter. This was the place.

It had taken seven long years, but he was finally ready to face Maya. He had a lot to apologize for. He waited a minute, gathering his courage.

Maya stood on the front porch sweeping stray fallen leaves from the wooden deck. A small boy Clay took to be her foster son, Tommy, and a little girl he assumed was his niece, Layla, were watching from their seat on a dark green porch swing.

Like Nicki, Maya had changed a lot. Gone was his gangly kid sister. In her place was a lovely young woman with short dark hair and a trim figure.

Catching sight of his vehicle, she stopped her work to stare at his truck with a puzzled frown. He opened his door, stepped out and walked to the front of the vehicle.

She dropped her broom. With a squeal of delight, she launched herself down the steps and into his arms.

Clay caught her up and swung her around laughing. Years of heartache vanished like smoke. Happiness nearly choked him.

Thank You, Lord, for giving me this moment.

As he set his sister back on her feet, she cupped his face in her hands. "I can't believe you're here. Let me look at you. You haven't changed a bit."

"You have. Talk about the ugly duckling turning into a swan."

"What?" She planted her hands on her hips. "Did you just insult me or compliment me?"

He grinned. "Go with the compliment angle."

"I believe I will." She threw her arms around him, and he returned her fierce hug. "It is so good to see you."

"Its good to see you, too, sis." She had no idea how good. Once more he saw how foolish he'd been to stay away. Oh, what his pride had cost him.

Maya released her bear hug. "Why didn't you call me and tell me you were coming?"

"I didn't have your number."

"That's right. I lost my phone in the tornado and I was using Greg's until recently. Well, you just hand over your cell phone and I'll add my new number for you."

"I don't own one, and I don't plan to get one."

"In this day and age you haven't found the need for a cell phone? That's nuts."

"I get along fine without one."

"That is caveman thinking."

He thumped his chest. "Uhg."

Giggling, she grabbed his hand and pulled him toward the house. "Come and meet the kids. Greg is out of town until next Monday, but I know he'll be excited to meet you."

Although Greg Garrison had been raised just outside of High Plains, Clay had little memory of him. Greg was several years older, and the Logan family hadn't traveled in the same social circles as the wealthy Garrisons.

On the front steps, Maya paused, looking at Clay intently. "You are planning to stay awhile, aren't you?"

"Actually, I don't have any plans at the moment."

"Wonderful. Then you're staying until I tell you to leave. You'll have to sleep on the sofa, but it's a comfortable one. We're in the process of building a new, bigger house, but it's far from done. Oh, I can't believe you're finally here. I'm never letting you leave again."

Chuckling at her high-handedness, he said, "I'm happy to be here, too, little sis."

She clapped her hands to her cheeks. "Thanksgiving! You *have* to stay until after the holiday. My whole family together, *praise the Lord*, that would be so wonderful. Have you been to the ranch?"

"Not yet." He was leaving his confrontation with his older brother until last. He strongly suspected it wouldn't go well.

Maya's frown returned. "But you will go see Jesse, right?"

"I'm not sure if that's a good idea."

Eyeing Clay intently, she said, "You'd better. You know he isn't going to make the first move."

"Same old Jesse."

"I don't think that's true. He's had a pretty hard time of it. Oh, but you should see his girls. They're as cute as a bug's ears."

"Cuter than this little honey?" he asked, winking at the doe-eyed youngster peeking at him from behind the porch railing.

"Layla, come say hello to your uncle Clay."

She shook her head.

Laughing, Maya scooped up her daughter, her eyes sparking with maternal pride. Layla hid her face against her mother's neck refusing to look at her new relative. "She's a little shy, but she'll warm up to you."

Turning to the young boy, Maya held out her hand. "Tommy, this is my brother, Clay. He's come all the way from Canada to visit us. Finally."

Clay extended his hand. "Howdy."

Tommy took it, and the two exchanged a hardy shake, then Tommy asked, "Is Canada a long way away?"

Thinking of the tedious hours he'd put in behind the wheel, Clay nodded. "It sure is."

"Did you happen to see a black and white dog, about this big on your way here?" Tommy held his hand below his waist. "His name is Charlie. He's wearing a red collar."

"No, but I'd be happy to help you look for him." Clay glanced at his sister, but she gave a tiny shake of her head.

Maya laid a hand on Tommy's head. "Charlie disappeared during the tornado. He and Tommy were very close."

It had been more than four months. If the dog hadn't come home by now Clay knew it wasn't going to, but it seemed Tommy wasn't ready to accept that.

The boy shifted away from Maya. "He'll come back. You'll see." Turning, he ran around the corner of the house.

Maya sent Clay an apologetic look. "Tommy was shuffled through four foster homes before he came to live with Greg and me. He was able to keep Charlie with him during every move. The dog was his only real family."

"Poor kid."

"Yes, which is why Greg and I are determined to adopt him."

"He must be happy about that."

"Actually, we haven't said anything to him so please don't. In case…you know."

"Gotcha. In case it doesn't work out."

"Right. What am I doing keeping you standing here on the porch? Come inside. Are you hungry? The kids and I just finished lunch, but I still have a half pot of chili simmering on the stove."

"You cook?"

She batted his arm. "What kind of question is that? Of course I cook."

"All I remember is your burned offerings. Burned eggs, burned pancakes, burned beans, burned meatloaf."

Pressing her hand to her cheek, she giggled. "Oh, the meatloaf. Do you remember how hard it was, and how Dad kept saying it was fine while everyone else was slipping pieces under the table to the dog."

"As I recall, Shep didn't touch them."

"It was years before I made meatloaf again for that very reason."

Still laughing, Maya headed into the house in front of him. Clay followed, amazed at how easy it was to fall back into the sibling banter they'd always enjoyed.

Inside, Maya lowered Layla to the floor, but the little girl clung to her leg while treating Clay to covert suspicious glances. After taking his coat and hat, Maya led the way to a cozy kitchen where the delicious smell of her chili set Clay's stomach rumbling.

"Have you had a chance to see the town," Maya asked as she withdrew a bowl from the cupboard.

"I did. It's hard to believe all the damage."

"You should have seen it that first night. I've never been so terrified in my life."

"I wish I'd been here to help."

After hesitating a second, she asked, "Why didn't you come back sooner?"

Was she asking about the storm or his original exit? He chose to talk about the twister. He didn't fully understand himself why he hadn't come back after his last fight with Jesse.

"I missed your phone call by two days. I'd just left the ranch to guide a group of hunters on a four-week packhorse trip. I called as soon as I got the message, but your phone was still out so I called Jesse."

"He told me he'd spoken to you. He told you about Marie?"

"Yeah. He mentioned the twister, but he didn't tell me the town had been leveled. Course, he never was talkative. I offered to come home then, but he said not to bother." Anger at Jesse's harsh words reared its head again.

"Jesse said that?" Maya was clearly shocked.

"Pretty much."

Ladling a heaping serving of chili into the bowl, she set it on the table in front of him and sat down. Sighing, she said, "There's a lot more to the story, but go ahead and eat."

Maya propped her elbows on the smooth pine surface and stared at him.

Tentatively, he sampled his first bite. The thick sauce and chunks of meat simmered to perfection with just the right kick of spices warmed him all the way to his toes. "Hey, this is good."

"Don't sound so surprised."

"But I am."

Rising, Maya picked up Layla. "Let me put this one down for her nap, and then we can talk."

Clay finished his lunch and sat back in the chair. It wasn't long before Maya joined him at the table again.

Sitting, she folded her hands in front of her. "Did Jesse tell you anything about the way Marie died?"

"Just that she was killed when a tornado touched down at the ranch."

"A tree fell on her car. It was the same storm that hit High Plains, but there was more than one tornado that day. Anyway, Marie wasn't at the ranch."

"Where was she?"

"On the highway a few miles from here. She'd left Jesse and the babies the day before the storm hit. Jesse found a note on the kitchen table along with her wedding band and the Logan family engagement ring. He was devastated."

Sympathy for his brother's loss and humiliation blunted Clay's anger. "I imagine he would be. I guess I can even understand why he didn't want to tell me about it."

"I hoped you'd understand. Their marriage wasn't happy, but everyone thought the babies would change that, including Jesse."

"She left her babies?" Even Clay was shocked by that.

"I really think she was suffering from some type of postpartum depression. I can't imagine leaving my child if I was in my right mind."

"Poor Jesse."

"In one of those bizarre things that happens in a twister, the kitchen was damaged, but the note and her wedding ring were still on the table. However, the Logan family ring was gone."

"That's a shame." The ring didn't have great monetary value, but to the Logans it was a priceless treasure. It had been handed down with love through the family for six generations.

"We all lost so much that night. Especially Jesse.

Losing the ring was like adding insult to injury. He feels so bad about it."

"You say the house was hit. How badly was it damaged?"

"It tore out the kitchen wall and took off a small section of the roof. The dining table Dad made for Mom was broken and Grandmother Logan's shadow box was smashed. I think I was as upset about that as I was about the ring."

Clay gestured toward her hand. "You can start a new tradition with your engagement ring."

She turned the diamond solitaire around on her finger. "I might just do that. I wish you could have been here for my wedding. Not that it was much, just a quick ceremony so we could get custody of Tommy…and all that other stuff that goes along with wedded bliss."

Her cheeky grin and sparkling eyes told him just how much she loved her new husband. Clay found himself looking forward to renewing his acquaintance with the man.

"I'm sorry I missed it, Maya."

"That's all right. You'll just have to be here when we renew our vows in the new Old Town Hall as soon as it's finished."

"I won't miss it. I promise. When's this going to be?"

Rolling her eyes, she answered, "Good question.

The hall is being rebuilt by volunteer workers and with donated supplies, but some of the work, like the electrical stuff, has to be done by professionals. It seems like every electrician and contractor in this part of the state has work backed up for months. That has slowed our progress."

"I can imagine."

"There was a lot of enthusiasm for the project when it was first proposed, but that has tapered off. People are busy trying to get their own lives in order, their businesses open and their homes rebuilt before winter. We meet on Monday evenings and Saturday afternoons now. Volunteers come and go as they can."

She glanced at the clock. "In fact, I'm volunteering there tonight."

"Doing what?"

"Whatever they need me to do. Hey, why don't you come, too?"

Nicki might have been the main reason he'd returned to High Plains, but helping the town recover had also been part of it. "Sure, I can drive a nail as well as the next guy."

"Great! And this way you can see some of your friends from the old days. Oh, wait!" Her smile vanished. She chewed the corner of her lip.

"What?"

"I just remembered. Nicki will be there tonight. Will that make it awkward?"

"Nicki and I have already run into each other."

Her faced perked up with special interest. "Really? How did that go?"

Nicki unzipped Kasey's jacket and handed it over to Josie at the day-care area in the annex building at the side of the church. The room, painted brightly with primary colors, had a separate play area lined with low shelves just the right height for an inquisitive toddler. Kasey, all smiles, waved at Josie. "Hi. Hi."

"Hi, Kasey. Are you ready to play with me?"

Kasey nodded and headed toward the toy she liked best, a red, white and blue plastic horse on wheels. Straddling the riding toy, she pushed herself across the carpet. "'Orsey. My 'orsey."

Satisfied that Kasey was happy and occupied, Nicki turned to leave. As she did, the door opened, and Maya Garrison walked in with Tommy and Layla. Behind them came Clay.

Once again, Nicki's breath caught in her throat. Heat rushed to her face as her pulse skipped into double time. Why did he have to be so good-looking? It wasn't fair that he could still turn her insides to jelly just by entering the room.

He nodded in her direction. "We meet again."

It had to be some kind of test. What was God trying to teach her? How to develop grace under pressure? Hadn't she learned that already?

Maya glanced from Nicki to Clay and back again. "I understand you've already run into my prodigal brother."

Nicki tore her gaze away from Clay and smiled at his sister. "Yes, we saw each other earlier today."

"Clay mentioned that. He's going to help with rebuilding the Old Town Hall."

"That's great. We can use all the help we can get."

Kasey came hurling across the floor and latched on to Clay's leg. Startled, he looked down. "Whoa, there, sugar face."

"'Orsey man. My 'orsey man. Hi." She held up her hand.

He shot Nicki an uncomfortable look. She supplied a translation of Kasey's babble. "'*Orsey man* is her word for cowboy. It's your hat."

He smiled down at Kasey. "So you like my hat, do you?"

Taking it off, he plunked it on Kasey's blond head and tipped it back so she could see out from under it. It was miles too big, but Kasey grasped it with both hands and tried to walk back to her pony.

Seeing that she was about to run into a chair, Nicki stepped forward, but Clay was faster. He scooped Kasey up, carried her to the riding toy and settled her in the saddle. Crouching beside her, he said, "Ride 'em, cowgirl."

It touched Nicki's heart to see the gentle way he

kept a hand on Kasey to make sure she didn't fall as she scooted her mount across the play area. After a few minutes, the little girl lost interest in the hat that kept falling over her face and let it fall to the floor.

Dusting off his Stetson, Clay settled it on his head and headed toward the door. Opening it, he nodded to Nicki. "Shall we go?"

He made it sound so personal, like they were going somewhere special together. There wasn't anything special between them. There never really had been or he would have come back years ago.

Walking past him without telling him required a force of will Nicki didn't know she possessed.

Clay caught up with her before she'd gone a dozen yards and fell into step beside her. She glanced over her shoulder, but his sister was nowhere in sight.

"Isn't Maya coming?"

"She told me to go on ahead. I think she needed to talk to Josie about something."

Great. Nicki resisted the urge to race toward the construction site. Instead, she tried to accept Clay's company as if he were any other neighbor. It didn't actually work, but she gave herself an A for the effort.

The wind had abated allowing the late-afternoon sunshine a chance to warm things up. The sunlight cast two long shadows in front of them as they walked eastward from the church. Nicki didn't need the visual evidence that Clay was beside her. Her nerve endings tingled with awareness of him. She knew exactly how it would feel if he were to take her hand and mesh his strong fingers with hers.

She shoved her fists deep into the pockets of her gray sweater-coat before she did something foolish—like reach for his hand.

"How long are you going to be in town?" she asked, desperately searching for something to say.

"I'm not sure."

Glancing his way, she caught him staring at her. What was he thinking?

She looked straight ahead. "I told you Maya would be glad to see you."

"You were right about that. She tells me you're the preschool teacher here. Screaming kids five days a week. How do you do it?"

"I scream back."

"I can't quite picture that. You used to have the patience of Job."

"Oh, how I wish that were true. Teaching can be trying, but it's also the most rewarding thing I've ever done."

They had reached the building. He stepped ahead and pulled the door open for her. "What does your husband do?"

"I'm not married."

Stepping inside the building, she noticed he hadn't followed. When she looked back, she saw a slow smile spreading across his features.

Chapter Four

Nicki wasn't married.

Clay couldn't believe how happy the thought made him. She didn't belong to someone else. He grinned as he followed her inside the shell of the rebuilt Old Town Hall.

The narrow-eyed glare she threw his way wiped the smile from his face, but didn't stem his curiosity. Where was her daughter's father? Was Nicki divorced? Widowed?

Just because she wasn't married didn't mean she wasn't seeing someone. He struggled to rein in his excitement.

No doubt Maya could supply him with the information he wanted. High Plains was still a small town. Not much went on that didn't become common knowledge in short order.

Only, he didn't want secondhand information. He

wanted to hear from *Nicki* about her life. They had been good friends once. God willing, she would think of him as a friend again someday.

Pausing inside the door, Clay surveyed the interior of the newly constructed building. Illumination came from the uncovered windows and a few work lights hung on exposed beams. Three tables had been set up in the middle of the floor. A half-dozen orange extension cords snaked across the floor to various power tools. The space smelled of newly cut wood, tar paper and sawdust.

Six people were already gathered in a group near the opposite end of the building. A blond, burly young man in a red plaid shirt seemed to be the site foreman, issuing jobs and instructions to the others. It took a second for Clay to recognize him as Allen Belford.

Allen had been one of the wild crowd Clay ran with in high school. They hadn't parted on friendly terms. The last time Clay had seen Allen both of them had been sitting in the High Plains police station. Allen had been nursing a black eye and split lip while Clay sported some equally impressive bruises and bleeding knuckles.

Because of Nicki.

Allen stopped in mid-sentence when he caught sight of Clay. The people with him turned to stare. Recovering quickly, Allen shouldered his way through the group. "Clay Logan, is that you?"

"In the flesh." Clay waited with a sinking stomach for the reaction to his presence.

"I can't believe it. When did you get back in town? How in the world are you? Where have you been?" Allen, grinning from ear to ear, held out his hand.

Clay grasped it and received a hearty shake. Any worry about his reception vanished when he saw the genuine welcome in Allen's eyes.

"I got back in town today. I've been in Canada."

"Canada? Doing what?"

"A little of everything, but most recently a wilderness packhorse guide."

"You always did prefer a horse over any other mode of transportation." Allen clapped Clay on the back hard enough to make Clay wince.

Glancing at Allen's tool belt, Clay said, "I never thought carpentry would be your thing. You were into electric guitars and loud amplifiers if I remember right."

Allen let out a jovial laugh. "I still strum a little on weekends, but for our church, not the rock band I once dreamed about. I'm an insurance broker."

His face sobered slightly as he patted the leather belt at his waist. "The woodworking is a hobby that's come in handy lately."

"So I've noticed. I'm really sorry the town was hit so hard, but it looks like you're making a comeback."

"Actually, I don't live in High Plains anymore. I

moved to Kansas City after I graduated from college. I started coming back to help with this restoration when Glenis Appleton called me a few weeks ago."

Nicki spoke up. "Mother has devoted an enormous amount of time and energy into seeing that the hall is done in time for Founders' Day. She's been fundraising, recruiting volunteers and haggling with suppliers for the materials we need."

"Glenis is a force to be reckoned with," Allen admitted.

"When my father was alive, the Founders' Day celebration was always one of his pet projects. He loved the history of High Plains. Mother's intent on seeing that tradition carried on. They were married in this building on Christmas Day."

"Which means we should get to work," Allen said, briskly. "I hear there are a couple more weddings planned for when this place is done. I don't want it to be said that I stood in the way of true love."

As soon as the comment left his lips, Allen's stricken glaze locked with Clay's. An awkward silence filled the air.

Clay glanced at Nicki and saw the puzzled look she was giving them.

"What do you need me to do?" Clay asked, defusing the moment.

Allen's smile returned, but it wasn't as bright.

"You can take your pick of jobs, but let me introduce you to some folks.

Leading the way to several other men, Allen said, "I think you might remember Michael Garrison. He's our minister now."

Clay did remember him. The fact that he'd become a minister wasn't much of a surprise. Michael, a cousin of Maya's husband, had always been the serious one.

Clay nodded in acknowledgment. "Reverend."

"Welcome back, Clay. Maya must be delighted."

"For now. I give it twenty-four hours before we're bickering like we did when we were kids."

A teenage girl with her light brown hair in two braids came bounding into the room and skidded to a halt beside them. "I'm ready to help, Uncle Michael, as long as I don't have to sweep up sawdust. I'm *sooo* tried of that yucky stuff."

Michael chuckled. "This is my niece, Avery. Avery, this is Clay Logan. He's Maya's brother."

A guarded look flashed into her eyes. "So, that makes you Jesse Logan's brother, too?"

Clay winked. "Guilty as charged."

She looked down abruptly. A hint of color stained her cheeks. "I'll go see if I can help Josie with the kids."

She headed out the door as fast as she had entered leaving Clay to wonder about her reaction. Did she have a teenage crush on his brother or something?

"Let me extend an invitation to services on Sunday. We'd be delighted to have you join us for worship." Michael's words caught Clay's full attention. He promptly forgot about the teenager.

The prospect of attending church was flat-out daunting. Clay slid his hands into the front pockets of his jeans.

He hadn't been inside a church since the funeral service for his parents. While he sat silently in the front pew staring at the twin coffins and listening to Maya weeping, he'd railed inwardly against God and all that religion stood for. He'd turned his back on God.

But under an icy lake, with his lungs screaming for air and numbing cold sapping his strength, Clay found Him again. God had given Clay a chance to redeem himself.

It might have been Clay's stupidity that cost his parents their lives, but Clay had been able to save one pain-in-the-neck little girl. God must surely have big plans for *that* kid.

In his heart, Clay knew his parents would say the scales had been balanced.

But was he ready to face God in His own house? Clay wasn't sure.

"Thanks, Reverend," he said, without committing himself.

As Allen made the introductions to the group, a woman with long red hair pulled back in a ponytail extended her hand. "It's nice to meet you, Mr. Logan. I took care of your nieces when they were in the NICU."

Nicki said, "Clay, this is my next-door neighbor, Lori Martin. She's a neonatal nurse."

He raised one eyebrow. "Neo-whatal?"

Lori laughed. "Neonatal. It means I'm a baby nurse. I take care of sick and premature infants. How are the girls? I really got attached to them when they were in our unit. I was so sorry to hear about the death of their mother."

"I haven't seen them yet, but Maya tells me they're cuties."

"When you do see them, give them a hug for me."

"Will do."

Nicki and Lori then joined two women beside the far wall and entered into an animated conversation.

Clay longed to spend more time with Nicki, and it was clear she wasn't feeling the same way. Simply because she wasn't married didn't mean she'd be interested in renewing their relationship. Besides, would it be fair to her? He wasn't even sure he'd be staying in High Plains. And Nicki had a child.

Of all the reunion scenarios that had played out in his head over the years, not one had included a third party in a high chair.

Clay turned his attention to Allen as the man took center stage again. "I was hoping for a few more bodies today, but I know most people are trying to get their own homes rebuilt or repaired before winter sets in. Those of you who made it, you have my thanks."

"And mine," Michael chimed in.

Allen rubbed his hands together. "Okay, Christmas is less than two months away, and our project is running behind schedule, but Glenis Appleton has found a contractor willing to do all the electrical and ducting work for us."

A brief cheer erupted from the volunteers. Allen grinned, but held up one hand. "He's going to cost a little more than we budgeted for, but she assures me he can get the work done in the next three weeks."

From behind Clay someone asked, "Is he reputable? I haven't been able to find a local electrical contractor who can start work on my house until after the first of the year."

"According to Glenis, he's got good references and they check out. He's just arrived from Arizona and is looking for as much work as his crew can handle. Glenis gave me a bunch of his cards to pass out. Maybe he can get to you after he's done here."

"That would be great. I don't mind paying more if he can get the work done fast."

"I agree. All we need to do is finish the interior work that still needs to be done and get the siding on outside. I think it will be easiest tonight if we divide into teams."

As Allen assigned townspeople into two groups, Clay found himself working with Nicki carrying siding to the rear of the building while Allen, nail gun in hand, waited for them. A forth member manned the table saw, cutting the boards into the desired lengths.

Nicki donned a pair of leather gloves she pulled from the pocket of her sweater and lifted the first wooden board from the stack. Clay took the other end and followed her.

He said, "I'm surprised they aren't using vinyl or steel siding."

"We're trying to re-create the original look of the building so we're using wooden lap siding."

"It may look like the hall Zeb Garrison and William Logan helped erected here in 1860, but it's never going to be the same."

"Some of it is. We were able to salvage the cornerstone from the foundation and some of the original wood flooring."

"Was that really worth the effort?"

"Of course it was." She scowled at him over her shoulder.

"Why?"

"Because it is."

So much for logic. Stopping where Allen waited,

Clay helped hold the siding in place while Allen nailed it with a rat-a-tat-tat of his air gun.

Looking from Clay to Nicki, Allen grinned. "Seeing the two of you together sure brings back some memories. Do you remember the trouble we got into after senior prom?"

Clay tipped his hat back. How could he forget it? The sound of hammering and saws faded as he thought back to the night he'd held Nicki close for the first time.

All through high school Nicki had been one of the "good" kids. To Clay, as the self appointed leader of the "wild bunch," she had always seemed out of his league. A girl too good to be true. Funny, pretty, smart and talented, she shouldn't have given a guy like him the time of day. But she had.

After his parents died at the beginning of his senior year, Nicki had been the one person who reached out and connected with him. She had been the one person who understood. Her own father, a respected and beloved local minister, had passed away from cancer two years before.

She seemed to know exactly how bereft Clay felt. From the first day she stopped beside his locker to express her condolences, their unlikely friendship took off.

He should have left it at that.

True to his careless nature, he soon thought he

needed more from Nicki than friendship. She finally agreed to go out with him as his date the night of the senior prom. He'd never been more nervous in his life than when he'd stood at her front door with her mother looking daggers at him.

"I remember that night," Clay said quietly.

From the blush racing up Nicki's face, he figured she remembered that night, too.

They were memories Nicki didn't want unearthed, but she could no more stop them than she could stop the wind that blew across the prairie. Clay holding her as they danced in the school gym festooned with balloons and streamers. That quiet walk along the banks of the moonlit river.

She could still feel the strength of his hand holding hers, the way their fingers fit perfectly together. They'd talked about everything and nothing as the glittering stars made their slow journey across the night sky.

Later, when they slipped into the secluded darkness of the gazebo, Clay had kissed her with wonderful tenderness. A tenderness that quickly bloomed into teenage passion.

Nicki pulled her mind from the past and let her gaze settle on Clay's face. If she had given into him that night would he have stayed in High Plains? Would they have had a life together?

No! Don't even go there.

She'd made the right decision all those years ago. She was proud of that fact. Given the chance, she would make the same choice again. Whatever reason Clay had for leaving, it had nothing to do with her.

When Allen finished securing the plank, Nicki dusted off her hands. "One down, a couple hundred more to go."

Striding away, she could feel Clay's eyes on her as she walked to the saw. He stopped close beside her as they waited for the boards to be cut. With a crew working on the remaining framing inside as well as the siding, the guy manning the saw was being kept busy. The screeching buzz of the blade made conversation almost impossible.

Grabbing the set of boards as soon as they were done, Nicki hoisted them under one arm determined to manage by herself. "I've got these. You get the next ones."

Clay caught the end of the boards as she swung around. "No, you don't. You'll hurt yourself trying to carry something this heavy."

"I can manage."

"With my help." Taking the weight a few feet back, he motioned with his free hand for her to start walking.

She had little choice but to do as he said. Once again, they held the opposite ends of the boards level while Allen nailed. As soon as her side was secured, she was off like a shot for another piece of lumber leaving no time to reminisce about high school.

She was halfway back with another board when Clay rounded the corner. He scowled at her, but she chose to ignore him. She felt him take the weight of the plank behind her. Only the fact that it required both of them to hold the siding in place while Allen made sure it was level and secure, kept her from leaving Clay to manage alone.

The two men exchanged knowing glances as Allen nailed Clay's side first leaving her stuck holding up her end while Clay came to stand behind her.

"So," he began. "How's your mother?"

"Fine." She didn't have to talk to him. All she had to do was work beside him.

"She never liked me much."

"My mother's a very wise woman."

Each pause in conversation was punctuated with the nail gun racket as Allen moved down the board making sure he secured it to a stud. Twice the air hammer misfired, and he started muttering under his breath.

Clay cleared his throat. "What's your little girl's name?"

"We call her Kasey."

Allen finished nailing and Nicki took off, but

Clay was ready for her this time. His long stride let him reach the lumber pile first.

"Where's Kasey's father?" he asked loudly.

"It's a long story," she shouted back. Shouting at him actually felt kind of good. It wasn't a very Christian thought, but she couldn't help it.

Picking up her end of the board, she marched toward the rear of the building jerking Clay along.

They met Allen coming around the corner. "This roll of nails is jamming. I'm gonna have to get another one. I'll be back in a few minutes."

As Allen walked off leaving the two of them alone, Clay pushed his hat back with one finger. "Looks like I've got time to hear a long story."

Nicki dropped her end of the board. "Are you sure you can stick around to hear the ending?"

He winced. "I'm not going anywhere tonight."

Fisting her hands on her hips, she asked, "And what about tomorrow?"

She didn't want to do this, but she couldn't stop herself. She'd stored up too much anger and disappointment to pretend any longer.

He tossed his end of the board to the ground then spread his hands wide. "Nicki, I've already said I was sorry. I don't know what else I can say."

"You can start by telling me why *my friend* didn't bother to call or to write in the last seven years. Hello! Have you heard of e-mail?"

"I wrote." His voice was barely audible.

She raised a finger and shook it in front of his face. "One stupid line on a postcard is not writing."

"Things got…complicated."

Throwing both hands up, she said, "No kidding. Welcome to life. That doesn't mean you ignore your family and your friends. Do you know how worried Maya was? How worried I was? I didn't know for months what had happened to you."

"Jesse knew."

"And all he would say was that you decided to move on. No explanation, no nothing. What happened?"

"Jesse and I—had an argument."

"You two had lots of arguments. What was so different about this one?"

"That's not important, anymore. What's important is that I've come back to tell you how sorry I am. To try and make things right. I acted like a jerk that night. I tried to push you into something you weren't ready for."

Crossing her arms, she tried to hold on to her anger but it began to fade. "Nothing happened. We were teenagers."

"Like that's an excuse. You were the best friend I ever had. You still are—bar none. You deserved better from me."

She relented slightly. "I was your best friend? Really?"

"And still are. Well, except for this mule in Canada named Sadie, but she has such bad breath."

Nicki pressed a hand to mouth to hold back a smile, but she couldn't stop her giggle. How could he make her laugh when she was mad at him? "Clay Logan you're incorrigible."

"So I've been told."

At that moment, Allen came back holding his nail gun aloft. "Got 'er fixed. Let's get rolling. We've got a lot of boards to put up."

Nicki bent to pick up her end of the siding. When she straightened, she found Clay leaning close. She breathed in his masculine, musky scent realizing once again just how much she had missed him.

"Am I forgiven?" he asked softly.

There was a time she would have forgiven him just about anything, but so much had changed. She had changed. "I'll think about it," she answered primly.

A sparkle glinted in the depths of his eyes. "That'll do for now."

Two hours of nonstop work later, they had laps within a few feet of the pitched roof when Allen said, "It's getting too dark to continue. I say we call it a night."

Climbing down from one of the step ladders they'd been using, Nicki rubbed her aching arms and nodded. As she walked ahead the two men, she heard Allen speak quietly to Clay behind her. "Can I have a word with you in private?"

"Sure."

Nicki caught Clay's eye. She said, "I'll be inside."

He nodded, and the two men faced each other in the growing dusk. She could just make out the somber set of Allen's face.

Wondering what they had to discuss that was so serious, Nicki rounded the corner of the building intent on giving them the privacy they wanted. She had only taken two steps when the sleeve of her sweater caught on a nail head protruding from the side of the building.

As she attempted to unsnag herself, she heard Allen say, "I never got a chance to apologize for my behavior the night of the prom, Clay. I'd like to do it now."

"My behavior was worse than yours."

Unhooking herself from the nail, Nicki should have walked away, but something in the tone of Clay's voice held her rooted to the spot.

"Nicki is a great gal," Allen said sincerely. "I was way out of line in the things I said about her. You were right to knock some sense into me. You've got a wicked left jab, by the way."

Clay and Allen had had a fight about her? Nicki frowned. When had that happened? What had prompted it?

"Did it get around?" Clay asked. "Did her reputation suffer?"

"A couple of the guys made some smart-mouthed comments, but I straightened them out."

Her reputation? That set Nicki back on her heels. She knew teenage boys sometimes bragged about their conquests, but it never once occurred to her that Clay might talk about their passionate interlude.

What had been said? If he had embellished the event at her expense, she was going to give him a piece of her mind.

Did it really matter? she asked herself. The whole thing had taken place years ago. Yet, it was one more piece of the puzzle that she'd been missing.

Yes, she decided, it did matter. Marching forward, she rounded the building and almost collided with Clay walking toward her. She brushed aside the hand he put out to steady her. "I think you have a little more explaining to do, Clay Monroe Logan."

Allen looked startled and guilty at the same time. "I thought you were inside?"

Clay didn't look the least bit put out. "Eavesdroppers rarely hear well of themselves."

She pushed her sleeves up above her elbows and clasped her arms. "My sweater got hooked on a nail and that's the only reason I overheard you talking about me, but don't change the subject."

He quirked one brow. "You weren't this bossy when we were in school."

"She's a teacher now," Allen said by way of explanation.

"Ah." Clay nodded in understanding.

"If you two were fighting about me, I deserve to know why."

Allen sidled past her. "Clay, I'm gonna let you handle this one."

When he was gone, she waited, glaring at Clay.

He grasped her elbow. "Take a walk with me."

As Clay's fingers wrapped around her slender arm, he was unprepared for the jolt that rocked him. The warmth and softness of her skin beneath his palm caused his heart to skip a beat before jumping into a rapid rhythm that stole his breath.

It felt a lot like jumping off a cliff.

"Okay." Her voice was low and husky.

Releasing her, he curled his fingers into his palms. She took a step back and pulled her sleeves down.

Clay began walking toward the park away from the lights of the hall and the church, and she joined him. Side by side, they followed the sidewalk that once led to the gazebo at the park's center.

Beyond the narrow grassy expanse of the park the river ambled past the town. A muddy ribbon of current dotted with eddies and swirls, it ran between deep, tree-lined banks except for where the path of the tornado transected it. The missing and broken cottonwoods gave mute testimony to the power of the storm that had run down the town, but the break allowed a clear glimpse of the water as it reflected the last rose and gold colors of the setting sun.

When they reached the bare patch of ground where the pavilion once stood, they stopped by mutual consent. Clay stared sadly at the empty octagonal space until Nicki spoke. "Of all the buildings the tornado destroyed in this town, I miss this old gazebo the most."

"Me, too."

"Did your fight with Allen the night of the prom have something to do with your quarrel with Jesse later?"

"You could say that."

"Don't be cryptic. You brought me here to explain, right? So explain."

"You're not making this easy."

"I'm sorry. It's just that I've wondered why you left for so long."

"Allen and a couple of his buddies saw us here that night."

Nicki pressed her hands to her cheeks. "Here? They saw us here?"

"Yes."

She spun around and walked a few paces away. Raking her fingers through her hair, she drew a long breath and blew it out slowly. "Oh, my. I will never be able to look Allen in the face again."

Clay crossed the space between them and laid his hands on her shoulders. "Nothing happened. They saw two teenagers making out and blew the whole thing out of proportion."

"Because I was a minister's daughter."

"And because I was the town bad boy."

"Great. So when did your fight with Allen take place?"

"After I took you home I wasn't ready to call it a night. I ran into Allen and a couple of friends at the pool hall. They made some remarks about you—I threw a few punches—the next thing I know I'm being hauled into the police station."

"And the police wanted to know what the fight was about. How many people thought that you and I…?"

She suddenly stepped away from him and threw up her hands. "No. Don't tell me."

He had to fight the impulse to reach for her. "The police called Jesse. He and I had a discussion after he bailed me out and took me home. After that—"

"You decided I was better off without you. I know, I read the postcard but I certainly didn't understand it until now."

"I thought a lot of people would be better off without me."

She stared at her feet. "So you made the decision for all of us."

"A man's pride is a tricky thing, Nicki. He can know that what he's done is wrong, but that pride keeps him from seeing how to change it."

Turning away from him, she stared toward the river, her shoulders hunched as if she were cold. He wanted to gather her close, offer her comfort, but he sensed she wouldn't accept it. Not from him.

Finally, she said, "I'm sorry for any part I played in your estrangement from your family."

"It never was your fault."

Nodding slightly, she turned away, "We should get back. It's past Kasey's bedtime. She gets cranky when she's tired."

He didn't want to go back. He wanted to repair their friendship, to undo the damage he'd done to her trust all those years ago. But like the gazebo she missed, he suspected there wasn't much left to salvage of that friendship.

Clay fell into step beside her until they reached the hall. Maya was waiting inside with her two kids and Kasey. True to Nicki's prediction, the baby was rubbing her eyes and fussing.

Layla was crouched in front of her stroller trying to get her to smile by offering her a small stuffed yellow duck. Kasey pushed her away and reached for Nicki instead.

Nicki picked her up and Kasey's arms immediately encircled her mother's neck. Nicki patted her back and crooned to her. "There, there, it's okay. We're going home now."

Kasey quieted at once, then reached toward the toy Layla was offering. Clay, seeing the discrepancy in their arm lengths, transferred the duckling from one to the other. Kasey took the toy, laid her head on her mother's shoulder and gave him a big heart-melting smile.

It seemed there was at least one female in the family he could charm. Too bad he couldn't charm both of them.

With only a brief goodbye, aimed at everyone in general, Nicki left.

Suddenly, fatigue sapped Clay's strength leaving him weary and feeling like he'd been dragged behind wild horses. It had been a long first day back in High Plains.

Nothing was like he thought it would be. He was almost afraid of what the next days would bring.

Chapter Five

Maya flipped on the overhead light. "You can't hide in here forever."

Clay threw one arm over his eyes. "I'm not hiding, I'm sleeping." At least he had been.

He'd used fatigue as an excuse to hang out alone all the previous day but apparently it wasn't going to fly two days in a row with Maya.

"You're going out to see Jesse today."

"I am?"

"Yes, you are. Do you want me to go with you?"

"What time is it?" He glanced toward the window. It was barely light outside.

"It's just after seven and don't change the subject. Do you want me to go out to the ranch with you?"

"What I want is for you to turn off the light and go away."

"Not gonna happen," Maya said briskly. "Rise and shine or I'll sic the kids on you."

He lowered his arm to glare at her. "I'm up. I'm up. How about a little privacy."

Wearing a white T-shirt and an old pair of sweat pants, he maneuvered himself into a sitting position and rubbed his scalp with his fingertips.

"Fine. But if you aren't in the kitchen in fifteen minutes, I'm sending Layla in with orders to jump on the sofa, even if you're still sleeping on it."

He was used to getting up early, but he wasn't used to his baby sister bossing him around. He honestly hadn't gotten much sleep. Mostly because he couldn't stop thinking about Nicki. Her face intruded into his thoughts every time he closed his eyes. He wasn't about to share *that* information with his kid sister.

Instead, he asked, "Does Greg know how mean you are?"

She laughed, a bright happy sound that made him smile in return. "Fifteen minutes."

Twirling about, she left the doorway and headed down the hall. The smell of bacon and cinnamon toast drifted in and made his stomach rumble. It was nice not having to cook over an open campfire for a change. It was nice not having to cook at all. Maya had turned into quite a good chef.

"She's not mean."

Clay looked up to see Tommy standing in the

doorway, a mulish expression on his face, his little hands clenched into fists at his side. It was clear he was ready to defend Maya's honor. Clay admired his attitude.

"She's not mean, but she has bossy down to a fine art. Does she tell you what to do?" Clay rose and stretched the kinks from his back. Maya's family-room sofa wasn't the worst place he'd slept, but it wasn't the best, either.

Tommy's expression relaxed as he advanced into the room. "Maya talks to me like I'm a grown-up. She doesn't yell at me like some of my foster moms did."

A knot of sympathy tightened in Clay's chest. According to Maya the poor kid had had a rough life. "So, do you like it here?"

Tommy strolled to the game table where a pair of action figures faced off against each. He picked them up and banged them together in mock combat. "It's okay."

Clay pulled a shirt and a clean pair of jeans from his duffel bag while keeping one eye on the boy. "Just okay?"

Tommy shrugged. "For now."

"Are you planning on going somewhere?"

"They move me around a lot."

Clay realized the little boy was afraid he'd be moved again and lose the family he was trying hard not to love.

"I've done my share of moving around," Clay said.

Tommy looked up from his toys. "You have?"

"Yup. Texas, Arizona, Utah, Montana, Canada."

"Did someone make you go all those places?"

For years Clay had blamed Jesse for driving him away. He sighed heavily. "The truth is—no one made me go."

"I can't go anywhere else until Charlie finds me. I check with Mr. and Mrs. Otis every day 'cause that's where I was living before the tornado. I think that's where Charlie will come looking for me, don't you?"

Clay didn't know what to say.

Thankfully, Maya's called out, "Tommy, breakfast is ready."

Tommy laid his combatants aside and rose to his feet, a look of defiance on his face. "You don't think Charlie is coming back. He will. You'll see. He's my best friend."

Clay stepped toward the boy and laid a hand on his shoulder. "I think Charlie is lucky to have a friend like you."

The tension drained out of the child. "Some of the kids at school make fun of me. I don't like it much."

"I'm sorry to hear that. I'll tell you a secret. I didn't like school much, either."

"You didn't?"

"No. I used to play hooky and go fishing."

"I like fishing. My dad used to take me."

Clay ruffled the boy's blond hair. "Maybe one of these days we can go down to the river. I once caught a fifty-pound flathead catfish at the east end of the park."

"Wow!"

"His head was this big around." Clay bowed his arms to indicate the size.

Tommy's eyes widened. "For real?"

"For real." Clay nodded toward the door. "We'd better go eat before Maya throws our food out."

"She wouldn't do that."

"She might. For real!"

Tommy grinned as he hurried out the door.

In the kitchen, Clay saw Layla was already at the table. Bright-eyed, she straightened when she caught sight of him. "Uncle Clay, sit by me."

"He's gonna sit by me," Tommy informed her.

"He's going to sit at the end of the table. That way he will be by each of you," Maya announced, thumping down a plate loaded with bacon, scrambled eggs and toast in the place she indicated.

Clay sat obediently, but winked at Tommy. He mouthed the word *bossy* when her back was turned and Tommy smothered a laugh.

Setting her own plate on the table, Maya glanced between the two. "What's going on?"

"Nothing," Clay and Tommy chimed in together as the phone rang.

Maya wagged a finger between the two of them, but all she said was, "Eat."

After answering the call and talking quietly for a few minutes, she returned to the table. Sitting down, she clasped her hands in front of her. "Tommy, is there something you forgot to tell me?"

"I don't know," he said slowly. He didn't look up.

"That was your teacher on the phone. You were supposed to give me a note about meeting with her today."

His silence was more telling than any excuse. He looked braced for the worst.

Sighing deeply, Maya said, "Clay, could I impose on you to take Layla to preschool?"

He perked up. Had he just been handed an excuse to see Nicki again? "Sure, I can do that. Does High Plains have more than one preschool?"

"We have two. Layla attends the one at the High Plains Community Church. She has to be there by nine."

Maya rose and laid a hand on Tommy's shoulder. Gently, she said, "Why don't we go in the other room and talk about why your teacher wants to see me."

Tommy laid his fork aside. "Okay."

When they left the room, Clay took a sip of coffee. "Layla, what's your teacher's name."

"Miss Nicki. Billy and Bobby Benton are in my class. I don't like them."

"Why not?"

"They laugh at me. Mommy found a baby for Miss Nicki. I want her to find one for me."

The abrupt change of subject baffled Clay for a second. "Honey, I don't think your mommy found Kasey."

"Yes, she did," Layla insisted. "After the tormadeo."

"Tornado."

"Yeah. Tormadeo." Layla took a big bite of toast.

Clay concentrated on finishing his eggs. He wasn't about to get into a conversation about where babies came from with a three-year-old.

When Maya and Tommy came back into the room Clay noticed the boy looked much less apprehensive. Maya patted his shoulder. "Finish your breakfast and go get your backpack. We have to get going. Layla, if you're finished eating, go get your shoes on. Clay, thanks for driving her. I'll see you later and I'll want to hear all about your visit with Jesse."

"I'll give you a blow-by-blow."

"Very funny."

Maya dropped to her knees to exchange hugs with Layla and kiss her goodbye. "Remember, Miss Linda is going to pick you up after school today because I've got to run into Manhattan. Clay, be sure and tell Nicki that."

He saluted sharply. "Miss Linda will pick up. Got it. Do I need to know who Miss Linda is?"

"She's a neighbor. Nicki knows her."

Tommy reappeared with his backpack. "Guess I'm ready."

Maya grabbed her keys and her purse. "Okay, we're off. Oh, wait. Layla's booster seat is in my car. I'll leave it out in the driveway for you, Clay. Can you disengage the passenger-side air bag in your truck?"

"My truck is so old it doesn't have a passenger side airbag."

She made a face. "Oh, well, that will work. Do you have my cell phone number?"

"Somewhere."

"I forgot you don't own a cell phone. *That has got to change*."

"Go. We'll be fine." He hoped.

With his sister and Tommy finally out the door, Clay poured himself another cup of coffee. When he turned around, he found Layla standing in the middle of the kitchen watching him. She had her shoes on the wrong feet and a book under her arm. He glanced at the clock. It was ten till eight. He had an hour to kill.

He pointed to her feet. "You've got your shoes on wrong."

"I like 'em like this."

"I think you should put them on the right way."

"No."

"I'll help you." He bent toward her.

"No! No! I want Mommy to do it." She scuttled out of his reach.

He held up his hands. "Fine. You can wear them like that."

Scowling at him from across the room, Layla didn't reply.

Clay sat back on his heels and glanced at the clock. 7:53 a.m. Nine o'clock seemed a long way off.

Nicki checked the clock on the schoolroom wall as she readied her room for her class. She had ten minutes before the horde began arriving. Although she enjoyed all her students, her morning class was her most challenging. Thankfully, she had no afternoon class today.

The outside door opened and she turned around expecting to see Reverend Garrison. To her stunned surprise, she saw Clay walk in.

"I brought Layla." He indicated his niece who came in behind him, a pout on her face.

Layla gave him a sour glare then turned to Nicki. "Mommy did find Kasey, didn't she?"

Nicki recovered her composure and smiled at Layla. "That's right. Your mommy and Greg found her."

"See." Layla made a told-you-so face at Clay.

His puzzled expression was almost comical as he looked to Nicki. "You're going to explain this to me, aren't you?"

"Layla, why don't you put out the painting smocks for everyone," Nicki suggested.

"Okay."

When the child was occupied, Nicki turned back to Clay. "Greg and Maya were looking for Tommy's dog a few hours after the tornado. They found Kasey near some abandoned cottages by the river. No one knew who she was. We still don't."

"Wait a minute. Kasey isn't your daughter?"

Taken aback, she said, "I'm her foster mother."

"But I thought—" He clamped his lips shut.

She stared at him in shock. "You thought what? That I had a child out of wedlock?"

His eyes shifted to Layla. "It happens."

Nicki pressed her lips together as her annoyance drained away leaving her embarrassed. She knew his sister Maya's story, knew how her fiancé had taken off when he discovered she was pregnant leaving her to raise their child alone.

Clay looked at Nicki. "My mother used to say that all children are a gift from God. She would have loved Layla no matter how she arrived."

"Your mother was a special woman."

"She was, wasn't she?" He suddenly seemed lost in thought.

"Yes," Nicki said softly. "I see her in Maya and in Layla, too." Reaching out, she laid a comforting hand on his arm.

He met her gaze. "I used to think she was just gone. Now, I know better. One day, I'll see her again."

"Yes, you will."

The smile that lit up his face touched something deep inside her. He covered her hand with his own. "Thank you."

"Like this, Miss Nicki?" Layla called out as she laid a smock on each chair at the activity table.

"That's great, Layla." Nicki withdrew her fingers. This wasn't the time or the place to examine her attraction to Clay.

Folding his arms, he said, "Are you telling me that no one has claimed Kasey in four months? That doesn't seem possible."

Leaning back against her desk, she debated how much to share about what she'd gone through since the day Kasey came into her life.

He settled himself on the corner of her desk beside her. "What's the matter?"

"Nothing. Why do you ask?"

"You've got that look in your eyes."

Tipping her head to the side, she asked, "What look?"

"The look that says you can't decide if you want to tell me what you're thinking or not."

"That's silly." She stared at her shoes.

"I used to know you pretty well."

"That was a long time ago."

"Some things don't change," he said softly.

She pressed her lips together. He couldn't do this. He couldn't waltz back into her life and turn it upside down. She wouldn't let his charm make her forget that he could be gone again at the drop of a hat.

"Everything changes, Clay. If you don't believe that you're only kidding yourself."

Tipping his head back, he seemed to study the ceiling tiles for a long moment. Finally, he met her gaze and nodded. "Point taken. So, why do you think no one has come forward to claim Kasey?"

"Oh, several people have claimed her. Once the news got out, the police and SRS had a number of people show up or call saying she was their child. But Kasey has a distinctive birthmark. A heart-shaped strawberry mark on her tummy. Only one person *claiming* to be her parent knew about it. That woman turned out to be someone who worked at the hospital where Kasey was taken after she was found. DNA tests ruled her out."

"What do the police think happened?"

"At first they thought she must belong to someone who was traveling through the area and was caught in the storm. The entire town and surrounding area was searched. They even called in divers to search the river. When they didn't find anything the authorities turned to the National Missing and Exploited Children's database hoping to get a hit."

"I take it they didn't find a match?"

"They ruled out numerous possibilities through DNA testing. She isn't in the system. As the weeks went by it began to look more and more like the tornado was incidental. The police think she may have been deliberately abandoned prior to the storm."

"Wow. High drama in High Plains. Will someone be able to adopt her?"

"There's no hard-and-fast rule for a case like this, but usually, if no family is found within four or five months, they try to place the child in a permanent home."

She looked at Clay. "I'm hoping to adopt her. I filled out the papers yesterday."

Nicki had shared that dream with only one other person, Kasey's social worker, Emma Barnet. Nicki hadn't even discussed it with her mother, so why had she shared it with Clay?

He cocked his head to the side as he studied her. "I think you'll make a great mother. It's clear you love her very much."

A blush crept up her cheeks at his praise. She was saved from further examination of her tumultuous feelings by the arrival of several of her students. Pushing off from the desk, she said, "Time to get to work."

Layla, pulling one of the new arrivals by the

hand, stopped in front of Clay. "Uncle Clay, this is Gracie. She's my friend. We're gonna paint with our fingers today, aren't we, Miss Nicki?"

Nicki smiled at the children. "Yes, we are. As soon as everyone is here."

"Will you paint me a picture?" Clay asked.

Layla considered his request, but Gracie said, "I'll paint one for you."

Frowning at her friend, Layla said, "I'm painting one for him."

"You can both paint one for me. Mind if I stay and watch?" He addressed the question to Nicki accompanied by one of his please-don't-say-no looks.

She tried to harden her heart against him. "It might disrupt the class."

"I've missed all of Layla's growing up. I'd like to make up for some of that lost time. I won't be any trouble. I'll stay in the corner as quiet as a mouse."

"All day?"

Raising one finger, he wagged it at her. "You can't scare me off that easily. Layla told me her class gets out at noon."

His beguiling smile and the barest lift of his eyebrow sent her good intentions out the window. "Oh, very well."

"You can sit with me." Layla grabbed Clay's hand and pulled him toward the seating area.

Seeing him position himself on one of the tiny

chairs at the edge of the room was funny enough that Nicki had to smother a laugh.

The morning routine got under way as she supervised the painting projects, kept the children focused on painting on the paper and not each other, and then hung the wet art work around the edge of the room to dry. After the art project came circle time, when everyone listened to a Bible story she had chosen for the day.

True to his word, Clay remained quietly observing the activities, but she was never able to forget that he was in the room.

Watching Nicki in her element with a room full of children was an eye-opening experience for Clay. He was amazed at how easily she averted squabbles, offered encouragement and praise to each child and still managed to look utterly adorable while she was doing it.

She had grown into a lovely, caring woman—who had made it pretty clear she had no intention of resurrecting their past relationship.

Everything changes.

With Nicki's comment in the back of his mind, he kept his attention focused on Layla. Although his original intention had been to go out to the ranch that morning, he didn't mind spending a little time getting to know his niece better. At least she was talking to him now and not crying for her mother.

He hadn't been lying when he said he regretted missing so much of her childhood. The more he watched her, the more she reminded him of Maya when she was little.

A lot of his memories of their childhood together were good ones. He'd forgotten that in the years he'd been running away from who he was and what he'd done.

He was sorry when the morning came to an end.

When Layla had been released to the care of Miss Linda and the others children turned over to their parents, Clay lingered in the classroom. Nicki moved about straightening chairs and replacing playtime toys.

He said, "You have quite a knack with kids."

"Thank you. Children are easy to love." She carried a set of books to the library shelf and replaced them.

"Nicki, why haven't you married?" The question popped out before he had time to think about it.

She turned to stare at him in open-mouthed shock.

"I'm sorry," Clay said quickly, holding up one hand. "That's none of my business."

The last thing he wanted was to push Nicki away.

"You're right. It isn't," she replied brusquely, turning her back on him.

He wished he could see her face, but settled for trying to make amends. "Put it down to my lack of social skills. I've been in the wilds of Canada too long."

"With only a mule named Sadie for conversation." It was clear she was trying to make light of the situation.

"Something like that."

There was a knock at the door and a young woman came in with Kasey in her arms. "I heard the munchkins leaving and thought I'd save you a few steps by bringing Kasey here."

Nicki accepted the child from her arms. "Thanks Josie. You remember Clay Logan, don't you?"

Josie grinned and held out her hand. "I do remember you, but it's been a long time."

"A few years," Clay admitted as he shook her hand. "But you haven't changed a bit, Josie."

"Liar. Your sister must be thrilled to have you home. She's a great gal. I don't think Greg Garrison knows how blessed he is."

"If he doesn't, Maya will tell him."

"Josie runs the after-school program here," Nicki explained.

Clay glanced to where Nicki stood with Kasey in her arms. "That must come in handy. Thanks for letting me stick around during this morning's class, Nicki."

"You're welcome. Don't forget to take Layla's and Gracie's picture with you." Nicki pointed to the one still hanging on the wall.

"Everyone needs a little refrigerator art," Josie said with a grin.

He smiled, but his heart wasn't in it. He didn't own a refrigerator. He had nothing but the clothes in his duffel bag, a well-worn saddle, a few tools and a truck that had seen better days. Oh, sure, he had couple thousand dollars tucked away, but it wasn't much to show for seven years of his life. His lack of material possessions hadn't mattered when he drifted from place to place. It hadn't mattered until today.

Nicki held a place in the community. She had a job she loved. She had a child she loved even more and hoped to adopt. Her plans, whatever they were, didn't include a guy like him. He sure wasn't father material. He couldn't keep Layla entertained for an hour let alone help parent a child.

Old insecurities raised their heads. What was he doing here? He had no business trying to insert himself into Nicki's life? Helping rebuild High Plains and reconnecting with his family were the reasons the Lord had prompted him to come back.

Maybe.

What if he'd been wrong about that, too? What if none of this was what the Lord wanted from him?

Suddenly, his need to get away and think became

overwhelming. "If you'll excuse me, ladies, I have to get going."

With barely a nod, he rushed out the door leaving two startled women staring after him.

Chapter Six

"What got into him?" Josie asked as the door closed behind Clay.

"I'm not sure." Nicki turned away to gather her purse from the bottom drawer of her desk. Clay rushing out on her shouldn't come as a shock. He was just being true to form.

"I hope it wasn't something I said."

"Don't worry about it," Nicki sought to reassure her friend. "We'll see you tomorrow."

After leaving the school, Nicki stopped to pick up a few things at the store before heading home. When she pulled into the driveway beside her apartment, she saw her mom's car parked in the street.

Casting her gaze skyward, Nicki muttered, "Please, God, I'm not up to a round of drama with my mother."

Bracing herself, Nicki extracted Kasey from her

car seat and carried her toward the front door. It opened as she reached it. Nicki had given her mother a spare key shortly after moving into the apartment. Glenis took advantage of the fact to come and go as she pleased.

"Hi, Mom. What's wrong?"

"Nothing's wrong," Glenis replied with a tight smile. "I thought I'd drop by and see if you wanted to go shopping with me this afternoon. I didn't realize I'd beat you home from school. I hope you don't mind that I let myself in."

"Of course not." Nicki did mind, but knew it wasn't a point worth arguing about. Ever since her husband's death, Glenis had become overly involved in her daughter's life.

Kasey stuck out her hands and chirped. "Nana."

Glenis took Kasey who went to her happily. Nicki followed the pair into the living room. "I'd love to go shopping, but I can't."

Sitting on the sofa, Glenis released Kasey who scrambled down and headed for her toy box.

Nicki sank down beside her mother and sighed. "I've got the next unit's lesson plans to finalize and a ton of housework that needs to be done."

Glenis ran her finger along the top of end table. "Things do seem a little dusty."

Nicki rolled her eyes. "I've been busy."

"Spending time with Clay Logan?"

So *that* was what this impromptu visit was really about. "Clay and I both worked at the Old Town Hall the other night, but I'd hardly call that spending time with him."

"Yet he was in your classroom all morning."

Nicki shouldn't be surprised her mother was so well informed. Besides being on the rebuilding committee for the Old Town Hall, her mother was also the hub of a tight-knit group of gossips.

"Clay spent the morning with my class in order to get to know his niece better."

"Nicki, you need to watch out for that man."

"You act like he's an ax murderer."

"He's a drifter with no means of support. You father would never have approved of him."

"Daddy would have liked that Clay has come back to help rebuild the town."

"I wish I believed that was his only motive for returning. I saw the way he looked at you the other day."

"Don't make a mountain out of a mole hill, Mom. I'm not an impressionable teenager, anymore."

"But you can be rash and impulsive."

If her mother thought she was reckless, what would she make of Nicki's decision to adopt Kasey? Perhaps it was time to find out.

Drawing a deep breath, Nicki said, "I certainly don't think of myself as impulsive. I've put a lot of thought and prayer into what I want to do next with my life."

Eyes narrowed, Glenis demanded, "What does that mean?"

"It means that I've begun the petition to adopt Kasey."

Glenis sat back with a look of shock on her face. "You can't be serious."

"I thought you'd be happy. I thought you adored Kasey."

"Of course I adore her. She's a darling child. But fostering is one thing, tying yourself down for life with a child is something all together different. Being a single parent is no easy task."

"I think I'm getting the hang of it. Kasey's been with me for months now."

"You've become attached to her, that's obvious, but are you being fair to her, Nicki? Doesn't she deserve a family with two parents to love her?"

"She deserves to be happy and loved in a stable home. I can give her that."

"I assume you've made up your mind?"

"I have. I love her like my own child. We belong together."

"And what if her family is found after you go through with this? What then? I don't want to see you hurt."

Nicki embraced her mother. "I know you don't, but please say that you'll support me in this."

Glenis returned her hug. "I've always wanted what's best for you. I'm just not sure this is it."

Nicki sat back and struggled to hide her disappointment. Kasey toddled over to hand her the toys she held. "Bocks. Me bocks."

Smiling at her, Nicki nodded. "Yes, honey, those are your blocks. Show me the red block."

Kasey grabbed the correct color and held it up, a wide grin on her face. Sweeping back her foster daughter's fine, blond hair, Nicki said, "That's right."

Glenis rose. "Promise me you won't rush into this thing."

Looking up, Nicki saw the genuine concern in her mother's eyes. "I promise, but that doesn't mean I'll change my mind."

When the turnoff to the Circle-L Ranch came into view, Clay tightened his grip on the steering wheel to keep his hands from shaking. He was home. A place he thought he'd never see again.

The last time he'd passed under the archway he vowed he'd never come back.

Memories rushed at him so fast he could barely breathe. He saw himself sitting silent and filled with remorse in the front seat of Jesse's truck. His furious and just as silent brother was driving him home from the High Plains police station as dawn was breaking.

The heated words had come later. Clay struggled to block them from his mind.

Turning onto the gravel road, he tried to prepare what he'd say this time when he faced Jesse. Everything that came to mind seemed inadequate in the face of all that had happened.

Clay wasn't used to trusting God, but he prayed that He would deliver the right words when the moment arrived.

The butterflies in his stomach churned madly as he drove up and parked in front of the house. Stepping out of his truck, he let his gaze sweep over the place. The two-story stone-and-wood home built by his ancestors hadn't changed much. The broad porch that wrapped around the house still welcomed visitors and offered the perfect spot to sit and look out over the sweeping Flint Hills.

He could see the new repairs to the roof and kitchen wall. The path of the twister leading away from the ranch and out into the hills was still evident in the torn-up earth and stripped trees. It would take years before those signs were erased by nature.

The rest of the place, the barn, corrals and outbuildings looked in great shape. Jesse was a good steward.

Sucking up his courage, Clay climbed the porch steps and knocked on the door.

When a harried-looking young woman with long dark hair and a crying baby in her arms answered, it took him completely by surprise. Through the open entryway he could hear more crying.

"Yes? Can I help you?" She bounced the baby faster but the crying only escalated.

"Is Jesse Logan here?"

She blew out an annoyed breath. "I wish he were. He's at a cattle sale somewhere and he's late."

After all Clay's nervous anticipation Jesse wasn't even home. The tension drained out of Clay leaving him disappointed. "Do you know when he'll be back?"

"Not soon enough. Look, I'm busy. What do you want?" Her brusque tone shocked him.

"I'm Jesse's brother. I was hoping to have a word with him."

"Okay. Maya called this morning and told me to expect you, but that was hours ago."

Regaining his composure, Clay put on his most disarming smile and held out his hand. "I'm sorry for any inconvenience. I didn't know anyone was expecting me. I'm Clay."

"Mitzy. I'm the nanny."

"From the sounds of things I'm guessing it's a tough job."

Giving an abrupt exasperated sigh, she said, "You have no idea. I had no idea!"

"I've come a long way to see Jesse. When do you think he'll be home?"

"He called and said he was running late and that he'd be back about two. He's making *me* late. I was supposed to leave by now."

Clay glanced at his watch. It was a few minutes before one. He managed a wry smile. "Guess I'll wait for him if you don't mind. Is this one of the triplets?"

"This is Madison—I think. Today's my first day. The other one you hear is Brooke, and I'm sure Sasha won't be asleep for long. None of them have slept much today."

He leaned closer to see the child's face. "Hey, Madison, I'm your uncle Clay."

His niece didn't seem impressed. "Maya said they were cuter than a bug's ears."

Mitzy rolled her eyes. "My grandmother lives across the street from Maya. Granny's the one who convinced me to apply for this job."

He laughed. "I'm not sure she did you a favor."

She didn't smile. "That's the truth. I'm never having kids of my own."

Mitzy turned away and left the doorway. "Look, if you want to wait that'll be fine but I've got to feed this one. She's hungry—like her sister. This is *definitely* harder than what I signed up for."

Clay followed her inside. Although the place hadn't changed much on the outside, it was clear Jesse's wife had updated the interior to suit her own tastes. The stone fireplace still dominated the living room, but the furniture was more stylish than the well-used sofa and chairs he remembered from his childhood. At one end of the room, three white basinets were lined up. Hand-lettered cards taped to the end of the beds bore each girl's name.

Mitzy disappeared into the kitchen and came out with two bottles in her free hand.

"Here." She pushed the blanket-swaddled baby into his arms and handed him one bottle

He clutched them both. "Wait a minute."

With pure teenaged disdain, she said, "I need to take care of the one that's crying. Just feed her. Madison is a good eater."

Looking from the bottle to the baby, he realized he didn't have a clue where to start. His niece scrunched up her tiny face and started wailing again.

He followed Mitzy and tried to keep the panic out of his voice. "I don't know anything about feeding babies."

Mitzy barely glanced at him. She was busy changing the next triplet's diaper. "It's simple. You put the nipple in her mouth. Just be sure to keep it tipped so that she doesn't suck in air."

Gingerly repositioning the baby to get a straight shot at her mouth, he placed the nipple on her lips. For one second, she rooted wildly then latched on and began sucking eagerly. The noise volume dropped by half.

Clay grinned brightly at Mitzy. "She's taking it."

"That's what babies do." Picking up the lone squalling infant, Mitzy walked to the sofa, plunked herself down and started feeding the child she held.

Carefully lowering himself to a seated position on the other end of the couch, Clay kept his gaze glued to Madison. Suddenly, she sputtered and began coughing.

Yanking the bottle out of her mouth, he looked to Mitzy. "What do I do?"

"Sit her upright."

He tried, but the baby curled into a ball, and he nearly dropped her. He did drop the bottle. It rolled under the coffee table.

"Good grief." Mitzy laid her charge at the back of the sofa and took Madison from him. Lifting the baby to her shoulder, she gently patted her back. His niece's belch became a wet gurgle as she upchucked on Mitzy's shoulder.

"Ugh!" Mitzy held the baby away as formula ran down her blouse.

Clay froze, his eyes wide with disbelief. "I told you I didn't know how to feed a baby."

Tipping her head back, Mitzy closed her eyes. "This is totally gross."

Taking Madison to the basinet, Mitzy exchanged the baby's wet blanket for a clean one and then wiped at the smelly stain on her shirt.

When she was finished, she grimaced at Clay. "I'm really glad you're here because I have a date in half an hour and now I have to go home and change first. Tell Jesse I'll see him in the morning."

Snatching her purse from the end of the coffee table, she marched across the room.

Clay shot to his feet. "What? No! You can't leave them with me!"

He started to follow her, but stopped when he realized one baby was still on the sofa. It didn't seem safe to just leave her lying there.

Mitzy waved one hand as she disappeared into the entryway. "You're their uncle. You'll take good care of them. The formula for Sasha is in the fridge. Warm it in a bowl of hot water before you give it to her."

"Mitzy, please." He heard the front door slam. She really was leaving.

Unable to believe it, he scooped up the child on the sofa and deposited her in the empty basinet, then rushed to the door. Wrenching it open, he bolted down the steps, but he wasn't fast enough. She was already in her car.

He caught up with her and rapped on the window. "Mitzy, don't do this. I don't know anything about kids."

She rolled her eyes, then lowered the window. "Feed them and they'll sleep. I have to go. I told your brother there would be days when I couldn't stay late."

Raising the window, she put the car in gear and took off. Stunned, Clay stood in the drive watching until the dust settled. Gradually, the sound of crying reached him. His gaze settled on the open front door. What was he supposed to do now?

Raking a hand through his hair, he glanced skyward. "Lord, please don't do this to me. A little help would be a good thing right now. Send Mitzy a change of heart before she hits the highway, please."

Clay waited, but no Heavenly help appeared in the form of a remorseful nanny or anyone else. "Jesse is gonna kill me."

The crying from inside the house had risen in volume. With leaden feet, Clay climbed the steps. In the living room, he stared at the cribs where all three babies were now voicing their unhappiness.

He desperately needed help. He had no idea how to reach Jesse. Clay remembered that Maya wasn't at home so there was no use calling her. Turning around, he strode into the kitchen, located a phone book and breathed a sigh of relief when he found the number he was looking for.

Dialing it, he held his breath as he waited for Nicki to pick up. Would she come?

Chapter Seven

Before Nicki could knock on the Logan homestead door it swung open. A very panicked-looking Clay held it wide. Relief washed over his face at the sight of her. He grabbed her arm and pulled her inside. "Thank you, thank you, thank you. This has been the longest twenty minutes of my life."

"You're welcome, but I'm only here because of the babies." The last thing she needed was Clay thinking she'd come running whenever he called, but this definitely qualified as an emergency.

She brushed past him and made a beeline for the living room. Setting Kasey down on the floor with a blanket and a plastic cup of dry cereal, Nicki went to the first crib.

Clay, his hair mussed and a damp circle on his red, pearl-buttoned, Western shirt came to her side and gestured toward the occupant of the bed. "I tried to feed this one. I think it's Madison. Anyway, she hardly took anything and then she went to sleep. Now, she's fussing again. What's wrong?"

Nicki quickly check the diaper and found it dry. That wasn't the problem. "How much formula did she take?"

"I don't know."

Turning around in a circle, he located the bottle and held it up to read the markings. "About a half an ounce."

"Then I imagine she's still hungry."

Kasey hoisted herself to her feet and came to grab Nicki's leg. Scowling she said, "Baby cry."

"Not for long," Nicki assured her.

Pointing to Clay, she said, "Take a seat and try feeding her again. I'll see to the next one."

He held up both hands. "I've already made her throw up twice. I don't think I should try it a third time."

"She probably threw up because her tummy is so full of air from crying. I can't believe Mitzy Garnet just left you."

"You can't believe it? You should have seen my face."

She glanced sideways at him and struggled to keep the laughter out of her voice. He still looked shell-shocked. "I might have paid money to see it."

"Oh, ha-ha! Some day I'll take you out into the

Canadian wilderness and drop you off without a clue how to find your way home. Then we'll see how funny it is when the shoe is on the other foot."

Wrapping Madison snuggly in her blanket, Nicki picked her up, then pointed to the sofa. "Point taken. Now, sit. Feed her a little bit and then burp her. After that, you can feed her a little more."

"Okay, but if she pukes again—I'm done."

"Good grief, Clay. Babies spit up all the time. It's no big deal."

His brow furrowed with doubt. "They do?"

"Yes." She handed Madison to him along with a burp cloth, then moved on to Brooke. Sasha had somehow fallen asleep again in spite of the noise her sisters were making.

Nicki waited until Clay had taken a seat and then handed him the baby. "It works better if you sit her up on your lap."

"Why?"

"It keeps them from spitting up because their stomach isn't as scrunched."

"That kinda makes sense."

After watching to be sure Clay had Madison correctly positioned, Nicki turned her attention to Brooke. Within minutes, she had the second triplet swaddled and in her arms. Settling on the sofa beside Clay, Nicki began feeding her.

"Will you listen to that," he said in awe.

Puzzled, Nicki looked at him. "Listen to what?"

"Silence." Clay's relief was comical.

Giggling, she cast a sidelong glance his way. He was smiling at her with such warmth that she felt it all the way to her toes.

"Did I say thank you?" he asked sincerely.

"A few times."

"You can't begin to know how glad I was to see your face. Jesse is gonna think this is my fault. Maybe with you here he won't blow a gasket."

"I'm sure he'll understand when you explain."

"I'm not sure he'll give me a chance."

The tone of his voice made her realize how worried he was about the coming confrontation with his sibling.

She bit her lower lip as she battled a bout of indecision. The brothers' personal relationship was none of her business. Dropping the subject might be a wise move on her part, but something in Clay's demeanor wouldn't let her brush off his concern.

Nicki said softly, "You and Jesse must have had a pretty serious falling out to keep you away for so long."

"Yeah."

"Would it help to talk about it?"

He looked away. "I don't think so."

"Was it about me?" Nicki wasn't sure why she

needed to know. She shifted Brooke into a more comfortable position.

After a brief hesitation, Clay admitted, "You were part of it."

"Only a part?"

His eyes met hers. "I told you how my parents died, but I never told you the whole story. The night they were killed, Jesse caught me sneaking out of the house and tried to stop me. I blew him off and went with my friends anyway. That's why he hasn't been able to forgive me. If only I had listened to him."

"Oh, Clay." She wanted to throw her arms around him and hold him close. He'd been living in a cloud of guilt for so long.

He stared at the baby he held. "Are you sure I'm doing this right?"

"I'm sure," Nicki replied, giving him a chance to decide how much he wanted to share.

Clay began speaking again after a few seconds. "When I got hauled in by the police the night of the prom and they told me Jesse was on his way, I was terrified something would happen to him, too. You have no idea how relieved I was when he walked in. Unfortunately, he didn't feel the same way."

"You can't know that."

"Let's just say I'm a good guesser."

Nicki asked, "What happened after that?"

"It was nearly dawn by the time he bailed me out.

In the police station and on the ride back he barely spoke a word. When we got home, he went straight to the barn and started his chores. I could see how mad he was, but I followed him anyway. I wanted him to understand that I got into the fight because I was defending your honor."

"Although I don't approve of fighting, I do appreciate the chivalrous gesture."

That pulled a small smile from him but it quickly faded. "One second Jesse was pitching hay to the horses and the next second he exploded. He said it wasn't enough that my delinquent behavior led to Mom and Dad's deaths, now I'd dragged your good name in the mud and destroyed your reputation. He wanted to know whose life I planned to ruin next."

Her heart ached to hear the pain in Clay's voice. "People say things they don't mean when they're upset."

"He meant exactly what he said. I can still see the look in his eyes. He said if I wanted to live a self-centered, irresponsible existence I should do it where I couldn't hurt anyone else he knew or cared about. That's when I decided to leave."

Nicki understood what he must have been feeling. "Only the ones we love have the power to hurt us the most."

A far away look filled his eyes. "Yeah. Only the ones we love."

"I still don't understand why you didn't call or write to me."

"How could I justify my behavior? The longer I stayed away the harder it became to face what a mistake I'd made. Then my pride took over and I couldn't admit I'd been wrong to leave. In retrospect, I'm not sure I was wrong."

She frowned. "How can you say that?"

"Don't misunderstand me, I'm sorry for the pain I caused you and my family, but I think I needed to stumble and fall on a rough rocky road before I could begin to see the path God has laid out for me."

She remembered his bitter rants against her faith when they were young. "Are you on God's path now?"

Looking at her, he quirked one eyebrow. "That's a question we all have to ask ourselves, isn't it?"

His gaze dropped to Madison. "Do you think I should burp her yet?"

Nicki allowed him to change the subject. "Good idea. Let me show you how to do it with her sitting on your lap. It will save your shirts."

She demonstrated with Brooke how to support the baby's chin and chest with one hand while gently rubbing her back. Clay fumbled a little but soon had Madison in the correct position. Madison showed her appreciation by belching loudly. A tiny amount of milk rolled out the corner of her mouth.

Clay wiped the baby's lips. "Are you sure this is okay?"

Nicki smiled. "I'm sure."

"How did you learn this stuff?"

"Lori and the other nurses at the hospital taught me how to do a lot of things when I took my first foster child home. He was an at risk preemie who needed a lot of care."

"Wasn't it hard to take a baby home and then give him back?"

"Of course it was hard, but I knew going into it that he wasn't mine to keep."

"What will you do if you have to give up Kasey?"

A chill settled around Nicki's heart. "I don't know. I try to tell myself that I'll rejoice because it means she's be reunited with her family."

"But the truth is…?" he prompted.

She looked at Kasey playing at her feet and smiled sadly. "The truth is—it will break my heart into a million pieces."

Glancing at Clay through suddenly tear-filled eyes, Nicki knew he'd heard the catch in her voice. She looked down hoping he hadn't seen the way her eyes misted over at the thought of losing Kasey.

He said softly, "You love her. It's easy to see you're torn by that love. You want what's best for her—even if that isn't a life with you."

Meeting his gaze, Nicki realized the brash, reckless boy she'd known had changed in more ways than she'd given him credit for. He'd become an insightful man capable of understanding the feelings of others—a man willing to search for God's message in his life.

She pondered his transformation, but didn't say anything as they finished feeding the two children. By the time Brooke and Madison were done with their bottles Sasha was awake. Nicki rose to her feet. "Miss Brooke here is still wide awake. Can you hold her while I take care of Sasha?"

"If she doesn't pull any funny stuff."

Chuckling, Nicki pressed Brooke into the crook of Clay's left arm leaving the nervous-looking cowboy holding both girls. The picture was so cute she wished she had a camera to capture it for all time.

A photo of Clay to replace the one I threw away.

Ignoring the wistful thought, she picked up Sasha and carried her into the kitchen to fix her bottle. Kasey tagged along behind her.

At the sink, Nicki filled a bowl with hot water and set the bottle of formula in to warm. The sound of a vehicle pulling up outside drew her attention to the window. Hoping it was Mitzy returning, Nicki pulled aside the curtain. It wasn't the irresponsible young nanny.

Letting the fabric drop back into place, Nicki walked to the living-room entrance. "Your brother is home."

Clay was grateful he had a few moments to brace himself before Jesse walked in. Looking down at the girls he held, Clay studied their delicate faces. He could see traces of Jesse in the arch of Madison's brow and in Brooke's nose.

Did they look like their mother? He had no way of knowing. He'd never met her. He'd never even seen a picture of her. Knowing he had only himself to blame for the lapse didn't make it any easier to face his brother.

When Jesse walked in, he stopped short at the sight of Clay. His eyes widened in astonishment.

The changes in Jesse weren't nearly as dramatic as the changes in their sister, but Clay could see them. There were a few fine lines at the corners of his eyes that hadn't been there before. He looked older and he looked tired—as if the weight of the world rested on his shoulders.

Clay managed a nervous half smile. "Hi."

For an instant, he thought he saw joy in Jesse's eyes. The fleeting emotion vanished to be replaced by a carefully guarded expression. "Hi."

They simply stared at each other for several long seconds, then Jesse asked, "What are you doing here?"

Clay tucked his disappointment deep inside. It had been too much to hope that his brother would greet him the way Maya had. "I decided it was past time for a visit."

Jesse's jaw worked as he struggled with some deep emotion, but he didn't reply. Finally, he noticed Nicki standing by the kitchen door.

She lifted her hand in a brief wave. "Hello."

"Hi." Jesse looked more confused by the minute.

Nicki glanced between the two men. "I'm going to take Sasha to the bedroom and feed her if that's okay with you, Jesse."

"That's fine."

Nicki ducked back into the kitchen and returned with a bottle before heading off down the hall shepherding Kasey in front of her.

Jesse turned to Clay. "Where's Mitzy?"

"She sorta took off," Clay answered, waiting for the explosion.

Jesse's expression changed to a deep scowl. "What do you mean? Why'd she leave?"

Clay struggled to rise from the sofa. It proved difficult with a baby in each arm. "I assume she went home, but that's just a guess on my part. She said she was late for a date."

Jesse's eyebrows shot up. "She took off? She just left my daughters with *you?*"

Clay finally managed to gain his feet. "She

seemed overwhelmed and upset. I heard her say she'd see you in the morning."

"I had my doubts about her, but I needed to find someone quickly. She's the fourth nanny so far." Jesse's voice trailed off.

Then he seemed to gather himself. He stepped forward, took Brooke from Clay and carried her to her basinet. "How long are you planning on staying?"

"I want to be back for good, Jesse." Admitting it aloud for the first time made it seem possible.

"I hope you aren't thinking you can just move into your old room. I've already got a full house."

"So I see."

Clay walked to Jesse's side and laid Madison in her bed. As he watched his brother tenderly tuck the girls in, Clay found the words he'd been wanting to say. "I'm really sorry about Marie."

Jesse stiffened. "Thanks."

"I should have come back then."

"It wouldn't have made any difference."

"I know, but you deserved at least that much respect from me."

"That's big of you," Jesse countered dryly.

Same old Jesse. Clay had a hard time biting back a retort. Determined not to be the same smart-mouthed kid who'd so often goaded his brother into a slug fest, Clay turned the proverbial other cheek. "You've done a good job with the place. I had to look hard to see where the storm damage was."

"It took out part of the kitchen wall and roof." Jesse turned away from his now-sleeping daughters and walked into the kitchen.

Clay followed with a glimmer of hope in his heart. It hadn't been a stellar welcome, but at least Jesse hadn't run him off the ranch. Maybe with a little more time they could mend their relationship.

Jesse motioned toward the outer wall. "I replaced the window and patched up the wall and roof but some things were destroyed beyond repair."

Letting his eyes rover over the walls, Clay realized what was missing. "Grandmother's shadow box is gone."

"I found it about a hundred yards out in the pasture smashed to pieces."

Clay came to stand at his brother's side. "What about her treasures?"

Grandmother's treasures had been a collection of mementos from all the generations of Logans who'd lived on the ranch. A silver baby spoon, a worn thimble, a small glass horse, dozens of items proudly displayed in a box lovingly crafted by her husband.

"I found a couple of pieces," Jesse said, "but not many. I put them away in my office for safekeeping. I want the girls to have them one day."

Clay pressed his hand against the wall. "Remember

how we'd pull our chairs up in front of the box and rearrange all the items."

"You always wanted the <u>little black glass horse</u> to go on top."

"And you thought the tin type of great-great—how many greats back was Grandpa William? Anyway, you wanted him to go in that spot."

Jesse folded his arms. "William Logan came West and started this ranch from nothing. He and Zeb Garrison founded the town of High Plains. He belonged on top."

Clay held up one finger. "Yes, but he rode in on a horse."

Jesse shook his head in disgust. "You haven't changed. Everything's still a joke to you."

"Not everything." Reconciling with Jesse wasn't a joke but Clay could see it wasn't going to be easy. When Jesse made up his mind he seldom changed it, and he'd made up his mind years ago that his younger brother was just about worthless.

"Do you mind if I take a look around the place?" Clay asked.

"Suit yourself. In case you've forgotten, a third of the ranch still belongs to you. Don't worry, I've been paying the taxes, managing the cattle, doing the upkeep on the house and outbuilding. If something doesn't suit your taste, just let me know."

"Jesse, please. I didn't come here to fight."

Rocking back on his heels, Jesse said, "Now that I think of it, it's a good thing you're here in person. Why don't we make it official? I'll buy out your third."

Clay blinked hard. "You want me to sell my share of the ranch?"

This was his home. The ranch was his birthright. In spite of his absence, he'd never even considered selling the land his parents and grandparents had owned before him.

"Why not?" Jesse countered. "I've been doing all the work. I might as well own all the property."

"I don't want to sell."

Jesse shook his head. "You are such a dog in the manger. You never cared about this ranch. All you ever cared about was having a wild time and it didn't matter who got hurt."

"I know I messed up, Jesse, but I'm trying to change."

Slowly, Jesse's defensive posture relaxed and his face softened. "I'd really like to believe that, little brother, but just saying the words doesn't make it so."

Nicki finished feeding Sasha but sat for a while on the corner of Jesse's bed. She could no longer hear the sound of voices through the closed door. Was that a good sign for the brothers' ceasefire or a bad one?

Either way, she couldn't stay in here forever.

Rising she opened the door and carried the baby back to her sleeping sisters. Jesse sat on the sofa sorting through a stack of papers. The dark look on his face kept her from asking about Clay.

"All the girls have eaten now, Jesse. Is there anything else I can do for you before I leave?"

"No. Thanks, Nicki. We'll be fine."

"Okay. What are you going to do about Mitzy?"

He blew out a loud slow breath. "I'm going to look for another nanny."

"She's young, but she has a good heart. Can't you give her another chance? Explain to her what she did wrong?"

"No. This was inexcusable. Any suggestions on who else might want the job?"

"Not off the top of my head, but I'll keep my eyes and ears open. Something will turn up. The right person is out there, Jesse. Don't give up hope."

He nodded, but didn't reply. Picking up Kasey, Nicki settled her on her hip and left the house. As she closed the front door, she prayed God would send someone special to love and care for the triplets…and for Jesse.

Descending the porch steps, she saw Clay leaning on the corral fence beside the barn. He stood with one boot resting on the lowest board and his forearms propped on the top rail. He'd donned his hat and his sheepskin-lined jacket, but even without the trappings of a cowboy he would look at home on any ranch. Perhaps it was because he had cowboying in his blood.

She hesitated only a second before approaching him. From the set of his shoulders he looked as forlorn as his brother. It didn't bode well for their reconciliation. She walked over to him.

"Moo-cow!" Kasey squealed, clapping her hands. Inside the corral were a dozen black Angus cows contentedly chewing their cuds and watching the humans with casual interest.

Clay glanced her way. "Did you get Sasha settled?"

"I did. They're all asleep now."

He held out a small photo. "I saw this blowing across the yard. Do you recognize them?"

She took the picture from his hand. The faded and water-splotched snapshot was of two young boys sitting on the seat of a tractor. "I don't. If you take it to the church, they'll add it to the lost and found items. Michael and Avery are cataloging everything that comes in and posting it on a Web site. Someone might come looking for it."

Clay took it back. "I wonder how far from home this traveled?"

"The tornados that day touched down over a twenty-mile area. There's no telling how far it came."

"Or how far the things missing from this ranch traveled. They look like brothers, don't they?"

She heard the sorrow in his voice as he stared at the photo.

"How did it go between you and Jesse?"

A wry smile flitted across Clay's lips as he glanced at her. "The fatted calf has nothing to worry about."

Reaching out, he lifted Kasey from Nicki and sat the toddler on the top rail so she could see all the cattle. Delighted, she jabbered away and kicked her feet against the wood.

"I'm sorry," Nicki said sincerely. It was sad on so many levels. Both Logan brothers had always been too stubborn for their own good.

"Don't be. I gave it my best shot."

"You're not giving up, are you?"

He shrugged. "To be honest, I'm not sure."

"You shouldn't give up. Nothing is more important than your family."

"Next you'll tell me time heals all wounds, the grass is always greener on the other side and a stitch in time saves nine."

"If you're going to make fun of me, I'm leaving." She reached to take Kasey from him.

"No. Please don't go. I'm sorry. I thought this would be easier, that's all. I thought I knew what God wanted from me, but apparently I'm wrong again."

She couldn't keep the disappoint out of her voice. "So you're just going to quit and move on? If your relationship with Jesse is important, don't you think it's worth a little work?"

"I don't want to give up, but I don't know what else to do. I tried to tell him I'm sorry, but he doesn't want to forgive me."

"Okay, I'm going to say this and you can get mad if you want, but this isn't about *YOU*, Clay. Jesse is at a very bad place in his life. Think of all he's been through. He doesn't have to forgive you and welcome you back with open arms in order for you to be a good brother. Just be there for him. Show up. Help out without asking for anything in return. That's what families do for each other."

Nicki held her breath hoping that what she said had gotten through. Clay's scowl faded as he considered her words. He stared at the photo in his hand. After a long moment of silence he looked at her. "You don't pull any punches."

"I'm surrounded by preschoolers all day. They'd eat me alive if I didn't know how to defend myself. Stop searching for *why* God brought you back to High Plains, Clay. His plan is beyond our understanding. You're here. Do something positive."

She lifted Kasey off the fence and carried her to the car leaving Clay staring after her.

Chapter Eight

The morning after his not-so-successful visit with his brother, Clay sat at Maya's kitchen table and nursed his second cup of coffee as he looked through the want ads in the local paper. The kids were at school and Maya had gone to work leaving Clay with nothing but time on his hands and Nicki's comment running through his brain.

Do something positive.

Besides the fact that Nicki's attitude had been a little hard to swallow, her advice wasn't as simple as it sounded. How could he help his brother if Jesse didn't want him around?

"It's not about me," Clay reminded himself.

Did Nicki really see him as that shallow and self-centered? Why shouldn't she? He'd never done anything to prove to her that he wasn't.

Concentrating on the paper again, he circled two

of the jobs that interested him. Both were ads for ranch hands. One was for-a-day rider work. The salary wasn't much, but he didn't need much.

The other one paid less, but offered room and board. If he took that job, he'd be working for the Rocking P Ranch—the spread that bordered the Circle-L to the west.

Rising, Clay rinsed his empty cup and added it to the top rack of the dishwasher. What he needed was a good long ride to help him sort things out. It always helped. The only trouble was, he didn't have a horse. Using his own two feet would have to do. Walking to the front door, he lifted his coat and hat from a hook, slipped them on and stepped out onto Maya's porch.

The morning air was crisp and carried the sharp smell of autumn. Fallen leaves lay in piles where they'd drifted into the street gutters. Frost decorated the windows of the cars and homes along the Garrison Street with delicate, sparkling patterns of ice. Winter would be here soon. The question was, where would he be when it arrived?

He didn't want to impose on Maya much longer. Although she insisted he wasn't any trouble, it was easy to see she had her hands full with her family and her job. And Jesse had certainly made it clear he didn't want Clay out at the ranch.

More than once in his wanderings Clay had lived

out of his truck, but that was less appealing than Maya's sofa. If he was going to stay in High Plains much longer, he needed to find a job and a place of his own.

Was he was going to stay?

Okay, Lord, You brought me here but I'm floundering. How about a little direction?

As Clay wandered the streets of High Plains, he surveyed the damage that still remained from the tornado. The majority of the city's trees and shrubs were bare of foliage, leaving the scars of the storm exposed. The town had been cleaned up, but it wasn't back to normal.

Some damaged homes still had tarps strapped across open areas of their roofs or walls. He passed at least four vacant lots where building hadn't been replaced. He tried to remember who lived in them, but couldn't recall the names or faces. It made him feel even more disconnected from the town he'd once called home.

Eventually, his stroll led him to the corner of First and Main Street. Maya would be at work inside the two-story Garrison Building, but Clay decided against stopping in. Instead, he headed west along Main inspecting the businesses that were the life-blood of the town.

The Pie Shop beside the Garrison building was open for business. The tantalizing smell of baked apples and cinnamon wafted out the door as a customer exited. Beside the bakery stood the High Plains Bank and Trust. It had suffered some damage to the ornate stonework on one corner of the building. A tall scaffold indicated that repairs were under way but he didn't see any workman. Maybe they were in the Pie Shop. That aroma would be hard to resist if a guy was working next door to it. Chuckling to himself, Clay kept walking.

The modern City Hall building sat in the middle the block between Second and Third. It had come through the storm with very little damage. Clay knew only too well that the city police station occupied the rear of the structure. He had no desire to see it again.

Past City Hall was a gapping hole in the line of buildings that fronted Main Street. The General Store that had occupied the spot since before World War II was gone. It was hard to believe something so much a part of the fiber of the city had been wiped away.

From the corner of Third Street, he crossed Main to the park and found himself once again drawn to the site of the gazebo. Of all the places in town that had been destroyed, Nicki said she missed the gazebo the most. Why?

Was it because their first kiss there meant as much to her as it had to him? He glanced toward the church and the annex building where Nicki would be teaching this morning. It was easy to imagine her surrounded by children and happily praising their efforts. She had a way with kids.

Something he didn't have.

As he gazed at the church, an elderly couple approached from the path that led to the river. Walking arm in arm with slow measured steps, they stopped when they reached the bare patch of earth.

The woman looked familiar, but it took a few seconds before Clay realized she was the woman in the photograph with Nicki, the one that had prompted him to come home. He tipped his hat in their direction.

The gray-haired lady sighed. "Isn't it such a shame?"

Her companion patted her hand where it rested on his arm. "It's just a place, honey. Folks are what's important."

"I know, but coming here always brought back such wonderful memories."

The man had been eyeing Clay. "You're one of the Logan boys, aren't you?"

"Yes, sir. Clay Logan."

"You're got the look of your granddaddy. He was a fine man."

"Thank you."

"I'm Frank Macer. This is my wife, Lois."

"Are you visiting family?" Lois asked.

"Yes, ma'am."

She nodded. "I'm sure that's a blessing after all that's happened. Maya is such a dear."

"Where'd you wind up?" Frank was clearly curious.

"Canada. I'm a wilderness guide there."

"Got out of ranching, did you?" Frank smiled. "Don't blame you. It's a hard life, but your brother seems to be doing okay."

"Jesse always had a head for it."

"It was a real shame about his wife." There was deep sympathy in Lois's voice. "Those poor babies. How is Jesse managing?"

He needs help, but he's too proud to ask. And he sure wouldn't appreciate me telling people he's having a tough time.

Clay glanced at the toe of his boot. "The ranch and the babies are keeping him busy. You don't happen to know of a nanny looking for work, do you?"

Lois tipped her head. "I believe I heard Clara Binter was looking for a job. Her husband passed away about a year ago and she said she was going nuts now that her last son has moved out. She raised five kids of her own, so she knows how it's done. I'll give her a call."

Clay smiled brightly and leaned toward her. "Jesse could use the help, but don't mention I said that."

She gave him a knowing smile. "Of course not. I understand how you men guard your pride."

"If you're tired of Canada, you should move back here," Frank said. "This town needs young people if it's gonna survive."

"I'll keep that in mind," Clay answered, his smile fading. While there were a lot of good memories for Clay in High Plains, there were a lot of sad ones he wasn't sure he could face on a daily basis for the rest of his life. Maybe thinking about staying was foolish.

Lois gestured toward the empty space in front of them. "I miss this old gazebo. It used to be a hub for the young folks."

"Maybe in our time, Ma, but not for this new generation," Frank scoffed. "They only like their phones and their video games."

She glowered at him. "You just don't like new things, Frank."

"That's right. That's why I keep you around. You don't have any buttons to push."

Lois batted his arm in mock disgust. "You mind your manners."

Rocking back on his heels, Clay said, "I have to agree with Frank. I don't even own a cell phone."

"Our grandkids take pictures and everything with theirs."

"Guess that's not such a bad thing," Clay admitted. "I wish I had a picture of this place before the storm."

Frank grinned at Clay and winked. "I don't need

a picture to remind me, I've got Lois. Why, I stole my first kiss from this old gal right here back in 1942."

Clay smiled. So he and Nicki hadn't been the first ones to take advantage of the privacy the little building had afforded. How many other romances had bloomed behind the lattice walls?

"Who you calling old?" Lois demanded. "You watch yourself, Frank, or you'll be fixing your own lunch."

Pressing a hand to his stomach, Frank said, "Speaking of lunch, Ma, we'd best get going. I'm starving."

She rolled her eyes, then smiled at Clay. "It was nice talking to you, young man."

He tipped his hat and they walked on, arm in arm, leaning on each other. A feeling of envy stole over him. What he wouldn't give to love and be loved for so many years.

Turning back to survey the vacant space the gazebo once occupied, Clay slowly stroked his chin. An idea began to take shape in his mind. He could rebuild the structure. He knew enough carpentry to take on the task. He'd worked one summer on a construction crew in Cheyenne.

He paced off the empty spot of dirt as he tried to recall how big the pavilion had been. It loomed so large in his memory that he had a hard time believing it had occupied such a small space. It had been about fourteen feet across he decided. Without a tape measure he couldn't be sure.

According to Maya, the town council didn't have the money to rebuild the structure. Would they object if someone else wanted to replace it? He couldn't see why they would.

He took a step back and settled his hands on his hips. He probably had enough money saved to pay for the materials. He'd stop by the lumberyard and get an estimate of what it would cost before he checked with City Hall to see if he could actually get started with the project.

Even if he left town later, he could still give the Macers and everyone in High Plains a new centerpiece for their park. A place for couples and families to gather. A place for future stolen kisses on prom night.

The thought occurred to him as he walked away that he'd also be leaving Nicki something to remember him by.

Leaving her preschool classroom at the end of the day on Friday, Nicki pushed Kasey's stroller ahead of her and crossed Main Street as she headed toward the grocery store. The cupboards weren't exactly bare, but she did need to stock up on a few things for the weekend and she needed to hurry.

The television weatherman had promised a balmy Indian summer afternoon, but as frequently happened in Kansas, he had missed the mark. Low, fast-moving clouds were rolling in. They carried the smell of rain.

Knowing winter would soon make it impossible to walk to work with Kasey, Nicki had jumped at the chance to use the stroller. Kasey loved riding in it—unlike her car seat. At times, Nicki thought she'd get a permanent case of whiplash from constantly checking to make sure Kasey stayed buckled up in the car.

Casting an eye toward the gray sky, Nicki shivered. She knew this wasn't the same kind of storm that had brought the tornado to High Plains, but like many people in town, she experienced a sense of dread whenever it became overcast. She'd never been frightened of thunder or the sound of the wind before—but that had changed.

Her shopping took only a few minutes. Leaving the store, she glanced as she always did toward the empty place in the park across the street where the gazebo once stood. To her surprise, she saw Clay unloading lumber from the back of a pickup and carrying it to the site.

Standing on the sidewalk, she battled the urge to cross the street and find out what he was doing. She glanced again at the clouds. The rain wouldn't hold off much longer. She needed to get Kasey home before they were caught in a downpour.

"Hello, Nicki." The sound of a familiar voice snapped Nicki's attention away from Clay. She realized she was blocking the door to the store and stepped aside to allow Mayor Gloria Dawson to go in.

Gloria, a woman in her sixties, was well known for her toughness and her gritty determination to see the people of High Plains recover from their disaster. Smiling, the mayor leaned down to speak to Kasey. "How are you, young lady? My goodness, you've grown in the past few months."

Nicki smiled with maternal pride. "She's not a picky eater. How are you?"

"I'm tired. I can't believe the red tape we're still coming up against after all these months."

Nicki nodded toward the park. "I see the city council has decided to replace the gazebo after all. I think that's wonderful."

"Actually, we don't have funds to cover that project, but Mr. Logan has applied for and was granted a permit to build it himself."

"Clay is doing that?" Nicki looked across the street in astonishment.

"With his own money. It never ceases to amaze me how people who haven't lived in High Plains in years have come back to help us recover. I'm proud to call this town home and proud to call the people who live here my friends. Such generosity really reveals the heart and soul of this community, don't it?"

Not only the community, Nicki thought. Such a gesture spoke volumes about the heart and soul of the man working across the street.

She'd accused Clay of making his return all about him. Had he taken her words to heart? If so, why rebuild the gazebo? Was it because of their kiss?

Nicki was tempted to cross the street and ask. But what if he was simply trying to restore some of the town's beauty and history and his gesture had nothing to do with that long ago tryst? If that was the case, she'd feel like a fool for bringing up the subject.

The first fat drops of rain began to fall making her decision for her. After saying goodbye to the mayor, Nicki hurried homeward, but found she couldn't stop thinking about Clay.

Not long ago, Nicki had dismissed her feelings for him as a lingering high school crush. That was still true. However, this new attraction she felt toward him was anything but girlish.

Chapter Nine

After dropping Kasey off with Josie at the church annex on Saturday afternoon, Nicki walked across the lawn to the Old Town Hall with mixed feelings. The day was overcast and chilly with persistent sprinkles of rain to make it feel even colder. The wind blew in fits and starts that sent damp brown and yellow fallen leaves scooting down the path ahead of her.

The dreary day matched her mood. She was worried about running into Clay again.

She wasn't sure how she'd face him or what she would say to him. Their last conversation hadn't been exactly kind on her part. It was bound to be awkward when they met again.

The sounds of hammering and the buzz of the table saw filled her ears as she stepped inside the building. The chill from outside lingered in the unheated space. She'd be glad when the electrician got the wiring and heating ducts installed.

Across the way, she saw her mother with Allen and several local men. They were all engaged in an animated conversation. Judging from the scowl on her mother's face, something wasn't going according to plan.

Nicki quickly scanned the room and groups of workers looking for Clay. To her relief, she didn't see him.

At least, she tried to tell herself she was relieved. Only, somehow, it felt more like disappointment.

"Hi, Nicki."

She jumped at sound of his voice behind her. Spinning around, she braced herself for his next comment, but he didn't say anything else. He just smiled as he walked by carrying a large tool box.

He didn't appear to be upset with her.

Why wasn't he? She'd all but accused him of being self-absorbed and shallow. Maybe he didn't care what she thought of him.

Even if he didn't, she still owed him an apology. She had no right to judge him.

Crossing the room, she saw Pastor Michael and his teenaged niece, Avery. Allen and Nicki's mother left the group they'd been talking to and came to meet them.

Allen said, "You've got your choice of projects,

folks. The plan today is to finish siding the east and south sides of the building, lay the tiles on the kitchen floor and begin work on the stage at the end of this assembly room."

"Is that where we'll be using the boards salvaged from the original structure?" Michael asked.

Allen nodded. "Yes. We're going to use them to edge the front and sides of the stage so they're in plain sight. One of the men has gone to pick the wood up from where it's been stored at Garrison's lumberyard. He should be back any minute."

Michael dusted his hands together. "I'll help with building the stage. The boards we were able to save were milled by the first Garrison to settle in High Plains. I think it only fitting his descendent help put them to use once again."

Allen clapped Michael on the shoulder. "I agree wholeheartedly. Nicki, do you want to work on building the stage or helping to installing the floor in the kitchen area?"

Nicki glanced to where Clay was carrying boxes of tile squares and a tool chest into the adjacent room.

"Or you can help me over in the church basement get sandwiches ready to feed everyone," Glenis suggested after following Nicki's gaze.

"I'll help you do that," Avery interjected quickly.

Glenis smiled at the girl, but Nicki knew it wasn't what her mother had been angling for.

"I guess I'll work on the kitchen floor. I'm too much of a wimp to work outside today," Nicki said brightly. In spite of her misgivings, she was dying to know what Clay had been doing since they parted ways at the ranch.

Clay reappeared empty handed and headed for the outside door. As he crossed the room, Michael motioned for him to join their group. Clay altered his path and stopped beside Nicki.

Michael said, "I'd like for us to pause before we begin our labors and ask the Lord's blessing on our work here today. Would everyone please join hands."

Already acutely aware of Clay's nearness, Nicki couldn't suppress the flash of delight that flooded her senses when his hand closed over hers with gentle strength. She chanced a peek at him, but his eyes were closed, his head bowed. She did the same.

"Heavenly Father," Michael began, "Your power and wisdom has carried us through our many trials, both as individuals and as a community. We humbly ask Your blessings as we continue the task of restoring this building. May it stand, not only as a reminder of our past, but as a symbol of our future, and of our abiding faith in Your goodness and mercy. Amen."

A chorus of "Amen," echoed around the circle. Clay's fingers slowly released hers. She didn't dare meet his gaze for fear her blush would give away her growing feelings for him.

Reckless, foolish feelings of attraction that had no connection to the real world. Clay was here today, but he could easily be gone tomorrow. If only she could trust him to stay.

As the group all went to start their assigned tasks, and Clay went back outside, Nicki's mother pursed her lips in annoyance. "Are you sure you don't want to help make lunches?"

Nicki forced a smile. "It doesn't take three people. You and Avery can manage."

Glenis sighed as a resigned look settled over her features. Reaching out, she cupped Nicki's cheek. "Yes, Avery and I can manage lunches. I'm more worried about how *you* are coping."

Nicki covered her mother's hand with her own. She knew her mother was referring to her feelings for Clay. "I don't have any illusions, Mom. My eyes are open."

"And so is your heart. I wish I could guard it for you."

"I'll be fine."

"All right, dear." Turning away, Glenis started to leave. At the door, she stepped aside as Clay came in carrying several boxes. He nodded in her direction, but Glenis didn't acknowledge him.

Nicki answered several queries from other women in the group about Kasey and then strode across the room. A sheet of plastic had been hung over the doorway between the main room and the kitchen area to keep the kitchen free of sawdust. As Nicki ducked under it, Clay looked up from where he crouched at the end of the room with a measuring tape.

"Would you mind writing this down? There's a notepad and pencil on the counter," he said with a jerk of his head in that direction.

"Sure."

He tilted his head to read the numbers on the tape. "Width seven feet, nine and one-quarter inches."

She added the numbers to the rough diagram of the room he'd drawn on the notebook.

He pressed the button and the metal ribbon hissed as it swooshed back into the case.

Pulling out a length again, he handed her one end and began backing across the room.

"I'm sorry, Clay," she said, quickly before she lost her nerve.

He stopped and looked at her intently. "Nicki, you never have to apologize for telling me how you feel."

"I could have been kinder in my choice of words."

"You meant well. At least, I think you did." A little smile played at the corner of his mouth coaxing a grin from her in return.

"Of course I meant well," she retorted.

His eyes narrowed to slits. "Promise you'll be nicer in the future?"

Her grin widened. "I rescued you from the triplets, didn't I? How much nicer do I need to be?"

He walked toward her allowing the measuring tape to retract. "That doesn't count. You only did that because you were afraid I'd drop one of them or mix them up."

"True. Okay, I promise to be nicer to you."

He pulled out a section of the measuring tape again. "Good. Hold your end against the far wall while I see how long this room is." He began backing up again.

Nicki did as he asked. When he pulled the tape taut, he took his reading. "Fifteen feet, four inches."

After writing it down, she said, "I heard you've started rebuilding the gazebo."

"Yup."

"By yourself?"

"Tommy is helping me."

The urge to ask Clay why he'd chosen the gazebo was almost overpowering, but she wrestled it down. Looking at the boxes on the counter, she said, "Maybe you should have brought Tommy with you tonight. I've never done this before. Where do we start?"

"I've never done it, either. I say we start in one corner and work our way down the room."

Nicki opened the first box of royal-blue-and-white vinyl tiles that closely matched the pattern from the original hall. She pulled out a sheet of paper. "Here are some directions."

Clay walked over and yanked the paper away

before she could read it. "It's peel and stick. How hard can it be? One of your preschoolers could do it without reading the directions."

Snatching the sheet back from him, Nicki uncrumpled it and turned away so he couldn't grab it again. "We don't have a preschooler with us—unless I count you—so *I'm* reading the directions. I want to do this right."

"I thought you were going to be nice to me."

"And I thought you said I could speak my mind."

He huffed. "All right, but I bet it says peel off backing—stick to floor."

"It says sweep the area thoroughly and mark the room into four equal quadrants." She met his stare and said tartly, "It says to begin laying our tiles from the center of the room outward."

He stepped closer to peer over her shoulder. "It does?"

She pressed the paper flat against her chest enjoying their little verbal sparing. It felt like old times. "Do you have one of those line thingamajigs?"

Crossing his arms, he said, "There's not a single *thingamajig* in my toolbox."

"Maybe Allen has one. While you go ask, I'll *thoroughly* sweep this floor since most *men* don't know how to accomplish that."

"Remind me again how you were going to be nice to me."

"Are you feeling picked on?"

He wagged a finger at her. "I'm not above telling your mother how mean you're being."

Hugging herself, she mock shivered. "Ooh, I'm so scared."

"You should be," he shot back, but his grin belied any threat.

As he left to find Allen, Nicki chuckled. Clay had always been able to make her laugh.

Thank You, Lord, for letting us renew our friendship.

A nagging thought suggested her feelings for Clay were becoming stronger than mere friendship, but she chose to ignore it.

Locating a broom, she swept the floor quickly and finished just as Clay came back into the room with a chalk line reel. Working together, they soon had the floor marked into quadrants.

"So how do you want to do this?" Clay asked.

She studied the layout. "I think if each one of us works in our own area it will go faster."

He looked skeptical. "Maybe, but I think it will work better if you peel and I stick."

"Okay." She wasn't convinced, but she dropped to her knees and pulled a carton of tiles to her side. Clay knelt beside her. Lifting the backing from the first tile, she handed it to him. He placed it along the chalk line and pressed it into place.

He held out his hand. "Next."

Nicki rolled her eyes, but obediently handed him the next tile. After they had the first row in place, Clay's speed began to slow. It took him longer to get each tile positioned exactly how he wanted it.

Chafing at his turtle's pace, Nicki sat back on her heels, peeled a dozen pieces and lined them up around her being careful to keep the sticky edges from touching. Concentrating on his task, Clay unexpectedly leaned to one side and his palm landed in the middle of a waiting tile.

The look on his face was priceless. Her laugh sputtered out in spite of her attempt to suppress it.

Lifting his hand with the white square stuck to it, he held it toward Nicki. "Very funny. What do you think you're doing?"

She pressed her fingers together beneath her chin and shrugged her shoulders in apology. "You're going so slow. I just thought I'd get a few ready in advance to speed things up."

"I'm going slowly in order to do it right."

As Nicki pulled the tile loose, it left a coating of sticky residue on his hand. "Sorry."

He wrinkled his face in disgust. Nicki couldn't help it—she burst out laughing again.

Extending his hand with a growl like a horror movie monster, he reached for her. Squealing, she jerked back. The tile in her hands slipped loose and landed facedown on two others.

She pursed her lips. "Oops. That's not good."

"Nice going, butterfingers."

Her jaw dropped open. "It was your fault."

"Right. Blame it on me. Everybody blames Clay." He was trying to sound annoyed, but she heard the humor lurking in his voice.

Rising, he said, "Try and get those apart while I find something to clean this goop off my hand."

Working to pry the pieces apart, Nicki pulled and tugged without success. In the meantime, Clay had located a rag in his tool box by the doorway. Wiping at his palm, he turned and walked toward her. "Put some muscle into it."

"I'm trying." Nicki gritted her teeth and pulled harder. The sheets came apart so abruptly that one flew from her hand and skidded across the floor just as Clay took a step. His boot landed in the middle of it.

He looked down. Nicki could see the muscle working in his jaw, but he didn't say a word.

Biting her lip to keep from falling into a fit of giggles, Nicki focused her full attention on setting the remaining tile in her hands into the correct spot on the floor. After she pressed it into place, she chanced a look at Clay.

He met her gaze, one eyebrow raised in distain. "You did that on purpose."

She shook her head. "I didn't."

"I think you did." He advanced toward her with purposeful strides, the tile still adhered to his boot.

She knew that glint in his eyes. Nicki rose to her feet and took a step backward. "Honest, Clay, it was an accident."

Leaning down, he picked up a blue tile, then positioned it in his hand, glue side up, and advanced on her with it held like a whipped cream pie ready for launching.

With the wall at her back, Nicki was trapped away from the door and safety. She sidled away from him grinning from ear to ear. "You wouldn't dare."

A wide, ornery smile creased his face. "Maybe I will, maybe I won't. I'm thinking this stuff will be like bubble gum in your hair. Don't you have to use peanut butter to get that out?"

The Clay she remembered just might do it. She scooted in the other direction, then made a quick break for the doorway. She wasn't fast enough. He slapped the tile into the middle of her back as she ran past.

She skidded to a halt. "Ah! I don't believe you just did that. This is my favorite work shirt."

She tried reaching over her shoulder to pull it loose, twisting one way and then the other to no avail.

Laughing, Clay reached for her. "Here, let me help."

"No, thank you." She spun away from him.

"Seriously, Nicki, let me give you a hand."

Grasping her shoulders, he turned her around

abruptly. Nicki's foot landed on the corner of the tile still stuck to his boot. She jerked back, but her shoe came off instead of loose. She hopped backward on one foot, lost her balance and sat with a thud—right on the tiles she had unpeeled.

She looked around her in disbelief. Clay roared with laughter and couldn't seem to stop as he doubled over with mirth.

Nicki tried to scold him, but found herself chuckling instead. Soon, they were both laughing like fools.

Offering his hand, Clay pulled her to her feet. Four tiles clung to the back of her jeans. He wiped the corner of his eyes with the back of his hand. "I'm sorry, but your expression was the funniest thing I've seen in a long time."

She looked over her shoulder. "I feel like a flattened armadillo."

He brushed back a lock of her hair. "At least you won't need the peanut butter."

His fingers lingered on her face. The humor in his eyes slowly changed to something deeper. With feather softness, he drew his fingertips along the curve of her jaw. He stared at her with an intensity that brought heat rushing to her cheeks.

She licked her suddenly dry lips. The movement drew his gaze there and he bent toward her.

Nicki turned her face aside to forestall his kiss and broke the tension between them.

As much as she longed to feel the touch of his lips on hers, she couldn't do it. She couldn't go down that road again. She wouldn't lay her heart bare and risk him breaking it again into a million pieces. It had taken her months to get over his leaving the first time.

Clay lowered his hand to his side, but didn't move away.

A rustling of the plastic drape announced the arrival of someone else. Nicki looked past Clay to see her mother enter the room with a plate of sandwiches.

Glenis stopped abruptly, her eyes narrowing at the sight of Clay and Nicki standing close together. "What's going on here?"

Nicki couldn't think of a thing to say.

Clay didn't bat an eye as he grabbed Nicki's shoulders and turned her around so her mother could see. Prying the vinyl square from the center of her back, he held it up and smiled at Glenis. "Someone's gonna need to order more tiles. Looks like we'll be short a few."

Chapter Ten

"Are you coming to church with us this morning?" Tommy asked from the doorway of Maya's family room.

"I guess so." Clay pulled on his second boot. A coat of polish had improved the worn, brown leather only slightly. Rising, he tucked his shirt-tail into his one and only pair of dress slacks. He rarely got dressed up, but today was an exception to the rule.

He still wasn't sure how he actually felt about attending formal church services. When he was outside under the open sky by himself it was easy to talk to God. Clay was just beginning to feel comfortable with those conversations. Would it feel the same when he was surrounded by a crowd of people?

Tommy ran his hand up and down the doorjamb. "Could you do me a favor while we're at church?"

The boy's overly casual tone caused Clay to look at him sharply. "Sure, if I can."

"Would you—ask God to bring Charlie back. God hasn't been listening to me."

The boy's sadness twisted Clay heart. He crossed the room to where Tommy stood. Dropping to his heels to place himself eye level with the boy, Clay struggled to find the right words. "God hears everyone, Tommy."

"I know, but I don't think I've been good enough. I was doing something I shouldn't have the day of the tornado and I think that's why God took Charlie away."

"The tornado wasn't your fault, Tommy, and neither was Charlie's disappearance."

"It might have been," Tommy insisted.

Clay clearly recalled the way he'd felt after his parents died. What could he say or do to change the Tommy's perception? He was a cowboy, not a counselor. Tommy, at his young age, had already seen more sorrow than any child should.

Clay prayed Maya and Greg would be able to give Tommy the love and stable home he deserved.

Laying a hand on Tommy's shoulder, Clay said, "When my parents were killed, I believed it was my fault. I thought God didn't care about me but I was wrong. He always cares about us, even when terrible things happen."

"That's what Maya says."

"My sister's a lot smarter than I gave her credit for." Clay leaned closer. "But don't tell her I said that."

A slight smile curved Tommy's lips. "I won't. Can we go fishing later today?"

"I'm afraid not. I've got a new job starting tomorrow and I've got to move out there today. We'll go fishing one of these days. I promise."

Tommy's smile faded. He nodded slightly. "I knew you'd be leaving."

The boy's fatalistic tone made Clay realize just how little Tommy expected from life. "I'm not going far."

"It's okay if you do."

Tommy turned away, but looked back over his shoulder. "Don't forget to ask God about Charlie."

Nicki made her way into the church sanctuary after leaving Kasey at the nursery. Sunday morning worship at the High Plains Community Church was normally crowded, but since the tornado, there was hardly an empty seat in the place. People in the town had turned to God in their time of trouble.

In spite of the packed assembly, she had no trouble locating her mother. Glenis always occupied the aisle seat in the third pew from the front.

"You're late," Glenis whispered as she scooted over to allow Nicki to joined her.

She could hardly be late if the service hadn't started yet. Keeping her comment to herself, Nicki sat down and picked up a hymnal. "Kasey poured her milk over her head at breakfast. I had to stop and give her a second bath this morning."

Soft organ music and the hushed atmosphere began to soothe the tension of her harried morning. Closing her eyes, she inhaled deeply and let the rest of her stress slide away.

When she opened her eyes, she saw the usher standing at the pew in front of her holding up two fingers and motioning someone his way. Maya shepherded her children in. Clay followed but there wasn't enough room to seat him with his sister's family. The usher then looked expectantly at Nicki. She in turn looked to her mother.

Glenis made room, but it was also clear to Nicki that she wasn't happy when she saw Clay standing in the aisle waiting to take a seat next to her daughter. She gave an audible huff.

Embarrassed, Nicki scooted over and Clay sat down. There wasn't much room. His shoulder and leg brushed against hers sending her pulse skittering into overdrive as currents of electricity darted along her nerve endings.

Clay leaned forward and nodded to her mother. "Morning, Mrs. Appleton."

Glenis inclined her head slightly but didn't reply.

He sat back, but after a few seconds he leaned toward Nicki and whispered, "Kinda chilly this morning, isn't it?"

She chose to misunderstand that he was referring to her mother's attitude. "It's not bad for the first week of November."

The organ music swelling to full volume signaled the start of the service. Nicki opened her hymnal to the page number listed on the music board. From the corner of her eye she saw Clay searching for a book but not finding one. What could she do but extend her copy in an unspoken offer to share?

His smile of thanks warmed her heart. It was a song they both knew well. Soon, the sound of his rich baritone blended perfectly with her alto and she relaxed.

All Clay's hesitation about returning to church faded away. It felt natural to be in God's house and singing the old familiar songs he remembered from his childhood.

Very little had changed inside the church in the years he'd been gone. The rich warm tones of the oak pews were complimented by the maroon carpet underfoot. The tall stained-glass windows glowed with shades of blue, red, yellow and royal purple. Overhead, heavy support beams arching upward to a wood-clad ceiling that always made him think of a boat.

The building hadn't changed. He'd changed. His faith had been tested by the death of his parents. To his shame, he'd failed that test, but God wasn't done with him.

As the service progressed, Clay listened intently to Michael Garrison's sermon, soaking in the words of scripture and finding an inner peace that had been missing in his life for a long time.

He glanced at the woman seated beside him. The light from the windows haloed her pale hair. She was wearing a turquoise sweater that brought out the blue in her eyes. Her face reflected a serenity he could only envy. Perhaps one day he would find the same tranquility in his relationship with God, but for now, it was enough to share this day with her at his side.

At the end of the service, they joined the throng moving toward the wide double doors at the front of the building. Keeping pace with Nicki, he hoped to spend a few more minutes with her outside, but she turned down a side hallway and entered the nursery. He was debating the merits of waiting for her when Glenis Appleton stopped beside him.

Primly attired in a navy dress with a wide black-leather belt, she studied him intently for a few seconds, then asked, "What has brought you back to High Plains after so many years, Mr. Logan?"

"God and a pickup truck." He grinned but she didn't smile in return. He should have remembered that Mrs. Appleton wasn't known for her sense of humor.

He wiped the grin from his face and cleared his throat. "My job in Canada had ended for the season. I heard about the town's rebuilding efforts and I decided I wanted to do something to help."

"Every spare set of hands is appreciated. I only wish things were progressing faster. I'm afraid we may not have the building completed in time for the Founders' Day celebration."

"Will it really matter if it doesn't get done by Christmas Day?"

"Of course it does. It's essential to the moral of the entire community. If we fail, we'll be handing this town one more defeat. That's something I won't allow to happen."

"Then I'm sure it will get done on time."

Crossing her arms, Glenis leaned back slightly. "I was surprised you didn't come home when Jesse's wife died. I'm sure your family could have used your support at such a sad time."

Clay realized a lot of people were probably wondering why he hadn't come home then. "I didn't learn of Marie's death until several weeks after the fact."

Glenis looked as if she didn't believe him. "Your brother is an extraordinary man. We all admire the way he managed to keep the ranch going after your parents died and took care of Maya. Now, taking care of those babies with his wife gone, it's simply remarkable."

Mrs. Appleton clearly saw Clay as the irresponsible Logan brother. It was hard to argue with the truth. "Jesse was always the one with a level head on his shoulders."

Just then, Nicki came out of the nursery holding Kasey's hand. Glenis looked from her daughter to Clay, then asked, "How long are you planning to be in town, Mr. Logan?"

The question for which he had no answer. Even if he wanted to stay, he wasn't sure there was a place for him here.

"I guess that depends," Clay said without taking his eyes off Nicki. If he stayed, could he become the kind of man she needed in her life? Was there a chance she could ever see him as more than a friend?

"I'm trying to convince him to stick around for good," Maya said as she came up behind them. Layla, giggling as she chatted with another little girl, headed outside.

Clay smiled at his sister. "Maya's mighty persuasive when she sets her mind to something."

"Yes, I am. Clay has hired on at Bill Porter's ranch, so you can see my influence is working."

Nicki's eyes widened in surprise. "You've taken a job locally?"

Did he dare read happiness into her look? "Bill needs a ranch hand for the rest of the fall calving season and I need to get off Maya's couch. He has a little house on the place that's furnished, so it worked out for both of us. At least, I'm hoping it will."

Glenis's eyebrows arched sharply. "You're not working with your brother?"

"No, ma'am."

Maya quickly interjected, "These days Jesse leases his pastures through the spring and summer months. He only has a small herd on the place and he can manage them by himself."

The fact that Jesse had sold off the herd their family had cultivated for generations and now rented out their acreage still rankled with Clay. It might have been a purely financial decision on Jesse's part, but it was one Clay didn't understand and would never have agreed to.

Nicki lifted Kasey to her hip. "I think it's great that you're thinking about staying in High Plains. The town needs more people in order to thrive."

The flow of worshipers filing past had dropped to a trickle. Clay motioned for the women to precede him out the doors.

The morning had warmed up beneath the onslaught of plentiful sunshine. The azure sky held only a few high wispy white clouds. True to form, the prairie wind tugged at clothing and carefully styled hairdos and sent the bare branches of the nearby trees waving softly.

On the church steps, Michael Garrison was busy greeting his flock. Around him stood several men and a woman with long, light brown hair and stunning green eyes. The warm glances that passed between the minister and the lady told Clay she was someone the minister held dear.

Glenis shook hands briefly with Michael and moved on to speak to several older women waiting for her at the bottom of the steps. Maya realized she was missing a child and returned to the church in search of Tommy. Nicki stayed by Clay's side.

Catching sight of Clay, Michael's smile grew bright. "I'm happy to see you accepted my invitation, Mr. Logan."

Clay settled his cowboy hat on his head. "Roping in a new sheep once isn't enough, Reverend. The hard part is getting that sheep to come back for more."

Michael laughed. "Are you saying my sermon wasn't good enough to coax you in a second time?"

"No, sir. I'm saying it was a fine sermon. You have a rare gift for speaking to the heart."

"Then you'll be back?"

"I will."

"Good. Let me introduce you to a few members of our congregation. This is my fiancée, Heather

Waters." Michael grasped her hand and she smiled sweetly at him before greeting Clay.

The two men, Clay discovered, were Colt Ridgeway, the police chief of High Plains and Silas Marstow, a local rancher. Clay recognized Silas as one of the men he'd seen working at the Old Town Hall and vaguely remembered him as being a couple of years ahead of him in school. Maya came out of the church, this time with Tommy in tow.

Silas said, "If you'll excuse me, I think I'll see if Josie needs any help getting the nursery straightened up."

As Silas reentered the church, Clay glanced at Nicki. "Is that the same Josie I met in your classroom?"

"Yes. She and Silas are engaged."

"Another happy couple?" Clay asked.

Heather said, "The tornado did a tremendous amount of damage, but it also revealed the caring nature of the people who live here. I'm not surprised a few romances have bloomed, or rebloomed as the case may be."

She fastened her knowing gaze on Colt. The police chief smiled in acknowledgment. The young woman standing next to him blushed a becoming shade of pink.

Clay glanced to Nicki for an explanation. Leaning close, she whispered, "Colt and Lexi were divorced but they're getting remarried in the Old Town Hall when it's done."

Quickly recovering his poise, Colt's steady blue eyes assessed Clay carefully. "Are you in town for long?"

That question again. Maybe he should print the answer on a sticky note and plaster it to his forehead. "I'm thinking about staying put, but I don't know for sure what I'm going to do."

Maya slipped her arm through Clay's. "This Thanksgiving will be the first time in seven years my family has been together for a holiday. Clay is hanging around until then if I have to hog-tie him to a chair."

"I'm only staying because your cooking has improved." Clay might poke fun at Maya's holiday plans, but a family get together was important to him, too. He needed another chance to mend things with Jesse.

Turning to Reverend Garrison, Maya said, "Speaking of Thanksgiving, I'd be thrilled if you could join us, Michael. As Greg's cousin, you *are* a part of the family."

Michael smiled at his fiancée. "Thanks for the offer, Maya, but Heather and I are taking my niece, Avery, home to visit my sister. Colt, what are you and Lexi doing for the holiday?"

A boyish grin appeared on the police chief's face.

"Lexi wants to have a big Thanksgiving with my family in the new house."

Lexi met his gaze with a look overflowing with love. "I had a solitary childhood. My parents were busy career people, so hosting a big family gathering is something I've always wanted."

Nicki smiled softly at Kasey. "Family is an important thing to us all. Perhaps that's the lesson God wanted the people of High Plains to remember."

Chapter Eleven

Nicki was disappointed not to see Clay at the Old Town Hall on Monday evening. Far more disappointed than she should have been, she finally admitted to herself later.

Later, alone in her bedroom in the small hours of the night, she faced the fact that her feelings for Clay were rapidly sweeping her into deep water.

Although she'd been delighted to learn he'd taken a job nearby, she also knew being a ranch hand was often seasonal work. It was no guarantee that Clay intended to settle down in High Plains. Even if she wished that he would.

"Which I'm not," she insisted aloud in the darkness. Rolling to her side, she plumped her pillow.

Pale moonlight filtered through the new curtains covering the window the storm had broken. The glass had been replaced, but her dresser top still bore a pair of deep scratches from that night. Even after all these months it looked bare without the collection of cherished mementos that had been destroyed by the fallen tree.

Her eyes went to the spot once occupied by her senior prom photo. A framed picture of Kasey sat there now. Kasey was the one she needed to concentrate on, not an old high school flame. Kasey needed stability. Clay had proven he wasn't about stability in the past.

A number of his daredevil pranks trickled through Nicki's mind. Had he really changed? How could she know?

She rolled back over and pulled the covers to her chin. Only time would tell. Until she knew for certain that he would make his home in High Plains, she would have to keep a close guard on her heart.

The following afternoon, Nicki saw Clay working on the gazebo when she left school. The weather had turned colder. For the most part, the skies had remained overcast. When the sun did peek out, it seemed thin and weak and failed to melt the sparkles of frost that lingered in the heavy shade of buildings and trees.

Perhaps it was the change in the weather that made her even more aware of her changing emotions where Clay was concerned.

Combating the urge to cross the expanse of the park

just to see the way his eyes lit up when he smiled at her, Nicki realized it was time to take a big step back.

Turning away from the gazebo without speaking to him, she made her way home to spend another sleepless night thinking about him.

The next day and the day after that, Clay was back again, working alone in the cold on the place that once meant so much to her. By Wednesday afternoon, Nicki admitted defeat.

She had called her mother to pick up Kasey from day care earlier in the day. Nicki's initial reason was that she needed to finish some paperwork after school, which she did, but it didn't take her long. Without a pressing need to get home, Nicki was free to check out Clay's progress.

He didn't notice her approach. Nicki stopped beside the growing skeleton of the structure and was once again reminded of the night she first kissed Clay—the night he vanished without a word leaving her heartbroken.

Turning her collar up against the chilly temperature, she said, "It looks smaller than I remember."

Clay glanced up from his work on the floor. "I'm using the old concrete footings that were left so it will be exactly the same size it used to be. It'll look bigger when the roof goes on."

"You've gotten a lot done. When have you found the time to work here? I thought you had a job?"

"Mr. Porter lets me off by about two o'clock if there aren't problems with the cattle. That gives me a few hours of daylight to work here or do other things. Some of the lumber cutting I've been able to do by lantern light out here in the evenings."

Nicki heard a shout. Looking up, she saw Tommy racing toward them. She nodded in his direction. "Looks like your helper is on his way."

"Greg and Maya have been letting him join me after school. The only thing Tommy wants more than to help is to remind me I promised to take him fishing."

By this time Tommy had arrived, out of breath and grinning broadly. "I'm here. Is it still too cold to go fishing?"

Nicki exchanged amused glances with Clay.

"Yup, it's still too cold," Clay replied. "The fish won't bite when the wind is in the north, but we're due for a warm up soon."

Tommy turned around and reached into his backpack. Pulling out a small black case, he held it up. "I almost forgot. Mom said to give you this."

Taking the leather pouch from the boy, Clay pulled out a red cell phone. He shook his head in disbelief. "Maya's bound and determined that I get one of these. I don't even know how to use it."

Reaching up, Tommy took the phone from Clay. "It's simple. You press this button to talk. This button shows you all the phone numbers you have.

Mom put them in. This button takes pictures and if you press this and then this you can take videos."

"Shown up by a tech-savvy child. You're making me feel old, kid." Clay snatched the phone back, placed it in the breast pocket of his shirt and fastened the snap.

Clay gestured to a stack of wood. "Why don't you start marking those cross pieces for me. I need them all five-feet long."

"Okay, Uncle Clay."

"I'll show you how to do the first one." Standing behind the boy, Clay hooked the end of the measuring tape to one end of the board and pulled it open. He pulled a pencil from behind his ear and made a mark. "It has to be right at sixty inches. Got it?"

"I got it." Tommy took the tape and placed the pencil behind his ear in imitation of Clay. The boy's serious face made Nicki smile. It was clear he had a whopping case of hero worship going on.

As Tommy began trying to measure off the wood Clay had indicated, Nicki studied them together. Clay was infinitely patient with the child's fledgling efforts. With gentle suggestions, Clay offered the encouragement that Tommy needed, helping him to use the tape that seemed to have developed a mind of it's own in the boy's inexperienced hands. It warmed her heart to see Clay's natural ability to connect with the boy.

Glancing up, Clay caught her staring. "Are you gonna just stand there or you gonna give us a hand?"

Smiling, she folded her arms. "I'm just going to stand here."

Tommy shook his head. "Girls don't like tools and building stuff. They just like dolls and babies."

Nicki could see Clay biting his lip to keep from laughing. Finally, he managed to say, "Tommy, could you get the drill out of the bed of my truck? I'm going to start fastening down the floor planks."

"Sure thing." Tommy took off like a shot.

"You're good with him," Nicki said.

"He's an easy kid to like. Do you know his history?"

"I know he's been moved from one foster home to another before ending up with Maya and Greg."

"The love they heap on that boy should give him a sense of stability, but Tommy isn't buying it yet. He's learned to expect the worst."

"He's certainly become attached to you."

Clay hammered a board into place. Looking up, he asked, "Do you know why?"

"Because you're a nice guy with new power tools?"

"No. It's because he has no expectations that I'm going to hang around. I'm safe."

"Are you staying?" she asked quickly then wished that she had bitten her tongue.

He stared at her for a long moment. "I'm not sure. I don't know what would be here for me if I did."

"Your family is here. Isn't that enough?"

Disappointment clouded his eyes. Had he been hoping for a different answer from her?

Hammering another board into place, Clay said, "Tommy's trying hard not to love Greg and Maya. He thinks something bad will happen to anyone he cares about."

His insight surprised her. "That's very astute of you."

"You're talking to a loner. I spent seven years trying not to love anyone or anything."

"Did it work?"

When he looked up, a touch of humor had returned to his eyes. "Not really. I fell pretty hard for Sadie."

Nicki knew he was trying to make light of his own struggle. She didn't press him. "Was that the mule with bad breath?"

"She had other good points that made up for that deficiency."

Shaking her head, Nicki held up on hand. "I'm not sure I want to know what they were?"

"She never kicked off her packs. That mule was worth her weight in gold."

Nicki glanced to where Tommy was shutting the truck door. "Did you notice that he called Maya 'Mom' when he gave you the phone?"

"I did. She'll like that."

Tommy returned and held up the cordless drill and power pack. "Can I do some drilling?"

Clay scratched his chin as he pretended to consider the request. Finally he nodded. "I'll let you drill some of the pilot holes."

"Cool."

Nicki smiled. "Then I shall leave you men to your work."

The warmth in Clay's gaze as it settled on her chased away the chill of the late afternoon. "Stop by anytime. I can always use some company. Especially yours."

Feeling foolishly lighthearted, Nicki turned around and started for home. Clay, it seemed, was rebuilding more than a gazebo. He was rebuilding her faith in him one small piece at a time.

The following afternoon, Clay boosted the first of the gazebo's lattice sides into place and fastened it with screws. One down, seven more to go. The design wasn't identical to the original, but it was as close as he could make it.

Taking a step back, he wiped the sweat from his brow and admired his handiwork. The sun shone bright and warm enough that he'd tossed aside his jacket and was working in his shirt sleeves. Today was definitely a nice change from the recent chilly, dreary weather.

Fall was one of the things he liked about Kansas. The long autumn often provided some beautiful crisp, days. Winter didn't usually get a good grip on the prairie until late December or January.

He heard the sound of running footsteps and turned to see Tommy dashing across the street headed in his direction. The boy skidded to a halt at Clay's side and dropped his backpack in the grass. "Wow, you got a lot done."

Clay glanced at his wristwatch. It was barely three o'clock. "Aren't you supposed to be in school?"

"We got out early 'cause the teachers have some kind of meeting. Do you think you could take me fishing today? You said we'd go when the weather got nice."

The boy's tone was so hopeful that Clay didn't have the heart to say no. "I reckon I've done enough work on this thing this week. Catfish for supper sounds good."

"Yeah!" Tommy shot his fist in the air as he jumped for joy.

Clay grinned at his enthusiasm. "Think we can rustle up some poles?"

"Greg has all kinds of stuff at his old place. He even has a kayak. For real. Maya says that's why Greg is building her a bigger house. So he has a place to put all his stuff."

"Then it sounds like he's the man we should see."

A half hour later, poles in hand, Clay and Tommy walked out of the Garrison Building. Greg had been only too happy to supply them with a pair of rod and reels and a tackle box. Clay had invited his brother-in-law to play hooky from work and join them, but Greg reluctantly declined. The two men had exchanged knowing glances. Clay understood that Greg wanted to come, but he was willing to let Tommy enjoy a boy's day out.

Clay had had his doubts about Greg Garrison when he first learned of Maya's hasty marriage, but Greg was proving to be a generous and caring man. Maya could have done a lot worse.

As Clay and Tommy paused on the sidewalk, Tommy looked up eagerly. "Can we go fishing where you caught that whopper?"

Looking toward the river, Clay decided fishing in the park seemed too tame. He had a sudden desire to see some of his old childhood haunts. One place in particular. The old bridge. "I know a great fishing spot, but it's quite a walk."

"I can keep up. I'm strong."

Patting the boy's head, Clay said, "I never doubted that for a minute."

Nearly three-quarters of a mile east of town, Clay led the way down a dirt road that skirted the edge of the river. Tommy, excited as a puppy, danced ahead of Clay, chattering away about the size and number of fish they were sure to land.

When they came to a bend where the road veered away from the water, Tommy stopped and pointed toward the river. "Is that the place?"

Clay shook his head. "Nope. We go cross country from here."

Crossing the weedy ditch to a barbed wire fence, Clay used his boot to hold down one strand. He wrapped his fingers around the middle wire and pulled up to make room for Tommy to climb through.

"Be careful, don't snag yourself," he cautioned. A second later he heard the sound of ripping cloth.

Tommy unhooked his pant leg and stood up. All the excitement leached out of his face as he fingered the tear by his knee.

He looked up at Clay and swallowed hard. "These are my new jeans. Do you think Maya will be mad? The foster mom I had before Mrs. Otis didn't like it when my clothes got messed up. She got real mad."

Pressing down both hands on the top wire, Clay swung his legs over and joined Tommy. "Did you cut yourself?"

"No."

Dropping to his knees, Clay inspected the rip. "As long as you aren't hurt, Maya won't be mad."

"Are you sure?"

Clay ruffled the boy's hair. "I'm positive. If you got hurt she'd be madder than a wet hen—at me."

Tommy relaxed. "Good."

Chuckling, Clay picked up the poles and rose. "It's not much farther and the big fish won't wait forever."

Tommy's smile reappeared. "Then we'd better hurry."

Moving ahead through the thick stand of trees that bordered the waterway, Clay said, "There's a railroad trestle up ahead. At least, I think its still there. The rail line was abandoned years ago, but they never tore down the bridge."

A hundred more yards brought them out of the trees and onto the bank where the rusting iron girders of the old trestle stretched out before them. Many of the wooden ties had rotted away leaving wide gaps.

"This is cool!" Tommy's eyes were round as silver dollars.

It looked even more dilapidated than Clay remembered. Only the massive concrete pillars in the water looked remotely sturdy. Sometime while he'd been away, the river had formed a sandbar island between the center ones. Saplings and shrubs had taken hold and formed a dense miniature forest among the fallen logs that piled up against the bridge footings during high water.

"How did you ever find this place?" Tommy asked.

"My granddad brought me and Jesse here when we were little. He liked to fish, too."

Happy memories enveloped Clay. He could almost smell his grandfather's cigar and hear his big-hearted laugh. Together, they all sat on this bank listening to the drone of insects, the chatter of squirrels and the hum of mosquitoes as they watched their bobbers not really caring if they caught any fish. It was enough to be sharing the time together. He and Jesse had been kindred spirits that day.

"I bet you came here all the time," Tommy took a step toward the edge of the bridge, but Clay grasped the boy's jacket.

"Whoa, partner, don't go out there. It's dangerous."

As soon as the words left Clay's mouth he nearly laughed aloud at the irony. The dangers presented by the old trestle had become a bone of contention between himself and Jesse. The summer of Clay's freshman year in high school, Jesse caught him and a couple of his buddies jumping off the rickety structure into the river.

That in itself had been bad enough. Adding in the fact that the river had been running bank full after a heavy rain had made it doubly dangerous. It was a wonder none of them had drowned, but Jesse's tongue lashing in front of Clay's friends had widened the gap that had always existed between the brothers.

It wasn't long before Clay found himself pulling other foolish stunts just to get a rise out of Jesse.

"Where are the big fish? I wanna put my line in there."

"I'd say right below us where the bank is undercut. Those old catfish like deep holes." Turning aside, he began to ready the poles.

Tommy took a couple of steps closer to the edge of the riverbank and peered over. "Hey, why is there a car down there?"

Clay's glance darted to the boy. "Step back, Tommy."

"But I can see the top of a car. It's blue." Tommy leaned farther out and pointed.

Clay pulled the boy back, then leaned over to check for himself. Looking down through the brush growing outward from the river's edge, he could make out the deeply dented roof and trunk of a late model hatchback. It wasn't a rusted out hulk as he had hoped. A sick feeling settled in the pit of Clay's stomach.

Grasping the boy's shoulders, Clay turned him away from the water. "I want you to go over and sit on that big log."

"Why?"

"Do as I say, Tommy," Clay replied sharply.

"Okay." Dejected, the boy walked over to a moss-covered fallen tree that lay about twenty feet from the river.

Using some exposed roots and flimsy sapling branches as handholds, Clay worked his way down the steep ten-foot embankment to the water. The vehicle was wedged under a tree that had fallen out from the bank. If the foliage hadn't been gone, Clay doubted anyone would have seen it.

His boots slipped on the muddy bank and he dropped waist deep into the chilly river but managed to grab hold of a branch. Gritting his teeth, he reached for the bumper and wiped the mud and moss from the license plate. It was a Colorado tag. The sticker in the left-hand corner showed the current year. The tag had been renewed in May.

His gaze was drawn to the submerged portion of the car. If anyone was still inside, they were far beyond his help. Working his way forward, he was able to see that the window on the passenger side was open, had been rolled down or broken. He could also make out what looked like the top of a child's car seat bobbing slightly inside the back. The rest of the interior was under water.

With a sinking feeling in his gut, he knew he might have solved the mystery of how Kasey came to High Plains. Turning away, Clay began to climb out of the water and up the bank.

Chapter Twelve

Nicki left her car with several others parked along the dirt road and followed the fresh tire tracks through the severed wires of a pasture fence. The sun was low in the sky, and the evening had grown chilly, but she barely noticed the cold.

Already a small group of people from town had gathered well back from the law-enforcement activity on the river. Word of the discovery had spread quickly. Nicki had learned about it from Mrs. Baker, the mother of the twins in her class. Her sister worked in the county dispatch office.

The muted hum of conversation stopped as Nicki approached the crowd. Standing apart from them, she saw Clay with police chief Colt Ridgeway near several police vehicles.

Clay caught sight of her and hurried in her direction. "Nicki, you shouldn't be here."

"Is it true?" she demanded. "Did you find a body in the river?"

Grasping her elbow, he led her away from the gawkers. "I found a car."

"Why didn't you call me? You know this could be Kasey's family."

"I wanted to wait until we knew something for sure. Right now, all we know is that there's an out-of-state car in the water."

Nicki curled her hands tightly inside her coat pockets. "Is anyone inside?"

"Divers have just gone in to check. It took a while to get the special water rescue and recovery team here from Manhattan." Clay laid a hand on her shoulder. "We'll know more soon."

She appreciated his offer of comfort, but she noticed how cold his hand was.

Suddenly, she became aware of the dampness of his clothes. "You're wet. You must be freezing."

"I'm fine."

Looking up at him, she asked, "What were you doing out here?"

"Tommy and I came out to do a little fishing. Don't worry," he added quickly, "one of the deputies drove him home. Tommy was thrilled at the chance to ride in a real squad car."

"Did he see anything," she asked, praying he hadn't.

"He saw the bumper of the car sticking out of the

water. I wouldn't let him come any closer once I realized what it meant."

Relaxing a fraction, Nicki stared at the men and vehicles lining the river bank. "At first, I prayed for answers about Kasey's family, but lately—I've been praying she could stay with me. I honestly thought someone had abandoned her. I was angry that someone could do that to a child. I was so sure they didn't deserve her. If they have been here all this time…" The lump in her throat kept her from saying more.

Police chief Colt Ridgeway walked over to them. "The divers say they're ready for us to bring the car out. We had to cut some trees away to get the tow truck in close enough."

"Did they say if there was anyone inside?" Clay asked.

Nicki tried hard to block the visions that filled her mind.

"There's one body still in the car. We think it's a woman."

The tow truck winch began to whirl. The cable screeched and creaked as it tightened.

Nicki glanced over her shoulder at the town more than a half mile in the distance. "Could the car have been thrown this far by the tornado?"

Colt shrugged. "Maybe. It's also possible it went into the water closer to town and was washed downstream. The river was rain swollen that night."

Nicki pulled her hands from her pockets and crossed her arms. "I thought you had divers check the river a few days after Kasey was found."

"We did. We just didn't search this far. It's fortunate that we found it at all. The divers tell me the car was hung up on a lip of concrete under the bridge. It wouldn't have taken much to break it loose and send it into a really deep part of the channel. If Clay hadn't come here fishing today, the car might never have been found."

The winch stopped when the vehicle had been pulled clear. Water streamed from the doors and frame.

Nicki turned away from the sight as nausea hit. Clay slipped his arm across her shoulders and pulled her close. "Take deep breaths."

She did, drawing in the warm, masculine scent of him until she regained some control.

Colt left them to return to the car where he and his deputies joined the sheriff and recovery team. Several of the men held up a large tarp to block the scene from view as a gurney from the coroner's vehicle was brought in.

After about twenty minutes, Colt returned. Nicki saw the answer she dreaded in his eyes.

She leaned into Clay's embrace, drawing strength from him. "It's Kasey's mother, isn't it?"

"We recovered a purse and we have an ID, but I can't give you the name. It will take a while to confirm the identity."

He wasn't telling her everything. She braced herself and asked, "What else did you find?"

Blowing out a deep breath, he said, "There's a child's car seat in the backseat. It's empty."

Nicki sniffed as sudden tears welled up in her eyes. "Kasey likes to unbuckle herself. I have a hard time keeping her strapped in."

Colt glanced toward the car. "In this instance, it may have saved her life. It's possible she was thrown clear before the car went into the water."

As he walked away, Nicki turned and buried her face against Clay's chest. "I'm going to lose her."

"You don't know that."

But she did. Once the deceased woman's identify was confirmed, her family would claim her little girl. In her heart of hearts, she knew the child she loved would be taken away.

Clay looked for Nicki at Sunday services, but she wasn't in church. He longed to see her and find out how she was doing, but he wasn't sure she would want to see him.

The discovery of the unknown woman's body had prompted a special prayer service the previous evening. A memorial had been started beside the church steps. The nook was filled with flowers, candles and cards.

Maya spoke to Josie after the service and reported back to Clay. It seemed that Kasey had developed a slight fever and Nicki had kept her home.

Although there was a storm of speculation swirling about the identity of the woman in the car, no one knew anything for certain. Colt had also been absent that morning, and Clay was forced to return to the Rocking P without any answer.

All the rest of the day, the need to see Nicki gnawed at his insides. After finishing the essential ranch chores, he had nothing to do and found himself pacing the length of the small living room in his quarters. Each time he passed the phone hanging on the wall, he started to pick it up but fear held him back.

What if the authorities had found Kasey's family and had taken her away from Nicki? How could he face her knowing he was responsible for setting that event in motion?

He could have taken Tommy fishing anywhere along the river. Why had he taken the boy to the old bridge? Only because he'd been eager to revisit some of his old haunts, to relive the thrills he'd once found there.

He should have been focused on the future, not the past. Torn between the need to be with Nicki and the uncertainty of her reaction in light of what had occurred, he found himself paralyzed with doubts.

He didn't make the call.

During his long hours in the saddle the next morning, as he moved the Rocking P herd to new pasture, Clay had plenty of time to rethink that decision. He'd grown more than fond of Nicki. His affection for her bore little resemblance to their high school attachment. His feeling went much deeper than anything he'd ever experienced before. They were rooted in his admiration for Nicki as a woman of faith and character.

Yet, underlying that realization was the persistent sick sensation that he was going to cause her pain—again. More than ever, he found himself doubting that he was on the path the Lord wanted him to follow.

By late afternoon, Clay's ranch work was done. As he stepped inside the lonely little stone house tucked into a shelterbelt of cedars, Clay realized he was hiding from his emotions the way he'd done most of his adult life.

Hiding hadn't been the answer then. It wasn't the answer now.

Besides, this is not about me.

It was about Nicki and what she was going through. He clapped his hat back on his head, turned on his heels and strode out of the house.

Thirty minutes later, Clay knocked at Nicki's front door and waited nervously for her to answer. When she did, he knew by the look on her face that the news wasn't good. His heart dropped to his boots.

He pulled off his hat and held it in front of him. "I just came by to see if you'd heard anything and to see how you're doing."

"I'm okay."

"You look terrible."

"You would have to tell me the truth, wouldn't you?" Stepping back, Nicki invited him in and led the way to the living room. She motioned for him to take a seat.

He said, "I just meant that you looked tired."

"I didn't get much sleep last night."

"How's Kasey?"

"She's better, her fever was gone by lunchtime."

Settling on the sofa, Clay turned his hat around and around in his hands. "What have the police found out?"

Nicki's voice quivered as she answered, "They've made a positive ID. It's Kasey's mother."

The pain in her voice made him long to wrap his arms around her and hold her close. "I'm so sorry."

After a tiny pause, Nicki continued. "Her name was Dana Cassidy and she was twenty-two years old. She's lived in Denver, but the authorities are having a hard time finding anyone who knew her.

Apparently, she moved around a lot. Kasey's name is really Katherine Cassidy. I've tried calling her that, but she doesn't respond to it. I don't know if I should call her Kathy or Katie, or if that will just confuse her."

"Have you learned anything about her father or Dana's family?"

"Dana wasn't married. Katherine's birth certificate lists the father as unknown."

He brightened. "That's good. I mean, if Kasey's father wasn't involved, you can still adopt her."

"I don't think I should hold on to that hope." She'd never sounded so lost.

"If only I hadn't gone to that bridge."

Smiling sadly, Nicki shook her head. "I don't blame you for finding Dana's car. I'm glad you did. She was someone's child, too. When the police locate them, they'll have some kind of closure. If you hadn't discovered the body, Kasey—I mean Katherine—would have grown up thinking her mother didn't want her and had simply left her by the side of a road. This is hard, but it's better for her."

"But not better for you."

"I'm learning to rejoice in each precious day Kasey gets to stay with me. When the time comes for her to leave, I won't be ready but I'll be prepared."

"You're a brave woman, Nicki Appleton. I want you to know how much I admire your strength."

"I'm not brave at all."

Rising, he tossed his hat aside and pulled her into his arms. "Yes, you are. You're very brave and very special. Kasey is blessed to have known your unconditional love even for a short time."

Nicki leaned into Clay's embrace. It felt wonderful to be held with such tenderness—to rest against his strong frame and not have to pretend she was all right. She was so tired of holding it together.

If only she could trust her heart to this man. She wanted to so badly. Unbidden, a tear slipped from the corner of her eye. She sniffed to hold back the threatening flood.

He lifted her face with a finger beneath her chin. "Hey, are you crying?"

"No." She sniffed again.

"Yes, you are."

"My eyes are just leaking."

He pressed her face into his shoulder. "That's okay, then. I don't mind getting wet."

"I'm so scared."

"I know you are, and that's okay."

"It's not. I should have more faith. No matter what happens, I know that it's God's will, but I don't want to lose her."

Drawing a steadying breath, Nicki pushed out of his embrace. The room seemed cold without his warmth. "I'm not going to start blubbering or I won't be able to stop."

"Tell me what I can do."

"You can pray for us."

"I've been doing that all along."

Rubbing her hands up and down her arms, she took a step away. Worry wasn't going to change the outcome for herself and Kasey. That was in God's hands.

It was time to give over those troubles to His keeping. Raking her hair back with her fingers, she inhaled deeply and blew it out slowly.

Forcing a smile to her stiff lips, she looked at Clay. "Are you going to work on the Old Town Hall project tonight or are you going to keep on with the gazebo?"

"I thought I'd give you a hand at the Old Town Hall. If you're going?"

"Actually, it's my turn to watch the volunteer's children. Josie and I trade off every few weeks."

"Babysitting has to been easier than putting up siding."

"Do you think so? Maybe you'd like to give me a hand with the group tonight."

"Me babysitting a bunch of kids? No. You saw me with Jesse's babies."

"You didn't do so badly. How are they?"

"Doing okay, I think."

"You haven't been back?"

"Not to talk to Jesse. I thought I'd give him a little more time to get used to my being around."

"Don't let too much time go by."

"I won't. Besides, Maya has this big shindig planned out at the ranch for Thanksgiving, so he'll have to talk to me then."

"A Thanksgiving reunion, that will be good for all of you."

Reaching out, he stroked his fingers down her face. "You're always thinking of other people."

Catching his hand, she held it to her cheek and closed her eyes. "Maybe that's why I'm such a mess."

He pulled her into his arms and rested his chin on the top of her head. "You're not a mess, honey, but even if you were, your friendship is still the best thing that's happened to me in a long, long time."

"I'm glad," she whispered.

Friendship had been the basis of the close bond they'd once shared. Nicki found herself hoping that it could become the basis of something more between them. Because as hard as she had tried to avoid it, she was falling head over heels for a drifter cowboy.

The patter of small feet hurrying across the floor signaled that Kasey had awakened from her nap. "Ni Ni, dink, please."

Nicki disengaged herself from Clay's hold and turned to her foster daughter, but Kasey barreled past to throw her chubby arms around Clay's leg. "'Orsey man. My 'orsey man. Me up."

Clay obeyed the order and lifted her into his arms. "Up it is, sugar. Are you feeling better?"

She nodded vigorously then patted his head. "Where my hat?"

"Is my hat missing? Where is it?" He spun around making Kasey giggle and clutch at his shoulder.

"Do you see it?" He twirled quickly in the other direction making the child laugh louder.

"There it is." He dipped Kasey low toward the sofa making her squeal. Righting her, he snatched up the hat and plopped it on her head.

Holding it up, she grinned at him and said, "More."

"No, that's enough spinning for a little girl who's been sick. We don't want Mommy to get mad at us."

Nicki's amusement faded, but she kept the smile on her face. As much as she wanted to be Kasey's mommy, she wasn't. Because of Clay's discovery— it was possible that she never would be.

Chapter Thirteen

Each day for the next four days, Clay finished his chores on the Rocking P Ranch as quickly as possible. After checking with his boss, he drove into town to work on the gazebo. With the roof finished and the six of the eight lattice walls up, it was beginning to look like the place he used to know.

Numerous townspeople had stopped by to express their thanks for his efforts, including the mayor and members of the town council. He had to admit it felt good to be included and accepted by the community that had once seen him only as a troublemaker.

With a little help from Maya, Clay had learned how to program the alarm on his cell phone. He set it for four-thirty in the afternoon—the time Nicki's last class let out. When the persistent beep in his pocket alerted him to the time, he put his tools away, crossed the park to the preschool and waited for Nicki outside her classroom door.

He knew she was going through a rough time, and he wanted to be there for her.

Each day, with no news, a little more hope returned to her eyes.

Today, she smiled softly when she caught sight of him and it lifted some of the ache from his heart.

"I'll only be a minute." She returned a large toy barn and farm animals to one of the many shelves in the room.

"How are you doing?" he asked, crossing the room to help her straighten up by pushing the little chairs under the work table.

"I'm fine," she replied without looking at him.

He moved to stand beside her and leaned down so he could see her face. "How are you, really?"

She pressed her lips together tightly, then said, "I'm a wreck. I dread going home. I just finished checking my cell phone messages and there weren't any. That's probably a good sign, isn't it?"

He lifted her chin with one finger forcing her to look at him. "It's going to be okay."

Grasping his hand, she held it pressed tightly to her cheek. "Keep telling me that. I need to hear it."

He prayed with all his heart that his words would prove to be true. He hated the idea that he'd had even an unwitting hand in making her suffer.

He slipped a comforting arm across her shoulder. Together, they left her room and followed the hallway to the church day-care area run by Josie.

As they neared the room, Clay's cell phone rang. He pulled it out of his pocket and saw a picture of Maya on the display. He flipped the phone open and answered it.

"Clay, have you seen Tommy today?" His sister's voice held a hint of worry.

"He came by for a few minutes after school, but said he wanted to go check with Mr. and Mrs. Otis to see if Charlie had come back." Clay had to wonder if the boy would ever give up on his missing pet.

"Thank you. I'll call there. Mrs. Otis is probably stuffing him with her oatmeal raisin cookies."

"Call me if you don't find him."

"I will. Thanks."

Clay ended the call but didn't close the phone. He hadn't realized Maya had added her picture along with her number. He glanced toward Nicki and tried to recall Tommy's instructions on taking pictures. Stopping in the hall, he said, "Hold on a second."

Nicki halted and looked back at him. "What are you doing?"

Raising the screen, he aimed it at her and snapped a photo. The image of her face remained on the display for a few seconds. It would remain in his heart for much, much longer. He pushed the button to save it. "Tommy was showing me how to use this thing. I think I'm getting the hang of it."

"They're great. I've taken tons of pictures of Kasey with mine." It was a pointed reminder to them both that she might not have the opportunity to take many more.

He aimed it at her again. "Try smiling this time."

She did. It wasn't an award-winning grin, but at least she didn't look so worried.

Two other women arrived at the day-care door ahead of Nicki and Clay. They entered the room to the happy shouts of their children. "Mommy! Mommy!"

Kasey hadn't seen Nicki yet. She was playing with her favorite toy, the plastic pony. Clay fumbled with his cell phone, managed to find the video button and began to record her singing a senseless tune as she rocked back and forth.

She looked up an instant later. A wide grin appeared on her face as she scrambled off the horse. "Hi. Hi, Mommy Ni Ni."

Nicki dropped to one knee and opened her arms. Kasey rushed to her and threw her arms around Nicki's neck.

Rising to her feet, Nicki held the child close. Love and tears glistened in her eyes as she turned to Clay. "Did you hear that? She called me Mommy. That's the first time, ever."

"I heard," Clay said, lowering the camera. A lump the size of Texas pushed up in his throat.

They belong together, Lord. Please don't separate them.

As soon as the other women and their children departed, Josie came over with Kasey's jacket and mittens. "Have you heard anything?"

Shaking her head, Nicki took the coat Josie extended and put it on the squirming child.

Josie looked at Clay. "It's been almost a week. Surely, if she had any family the police would have found them by now."

Although no name was mentioned, they all knew Josie was referring to Dana Cassidy.

"I'm trying not to get my hopes up," Nicki replied as she lifted Kasey and settled the child on her hip.

Josie smiled sadly. "We're all praying for you."

"I know that, and I thank you."

With her head down, Nicki turned toward the door. Clay held it open and followed her outside the building. In the parking lot, he waited as she settled Kasey in her car seat, then he held the passenger's-side door of Nicki's car open and extended his hand for her keys.

"You don't have to keep driving me home."

"I like the company. How often does a footloose cowboy like me get to spend time with a pair of pretty fillies like you two?"

"I hesitate to speculate, but I'm going to guess you've left a string of broken-hearted fillies behind you."

He shook a finger at her. "You've been talking to Sadie, haven't you?"

"Honestly, Clay, I'm fine. I can get myself home. I got myself here, didn't I?"

"You are *fine*. I hope you know that." He cocked his head to the side and wagged his eyebrows as he admired her trim figure in a dark red sweater that was belted at the waist above a narrow black skirt.

She shook her head at his foolishness. "Enough, Clay. Thank you for taking such good care of me this week."

"All right. You win." He closed the car door.

"How's the gazebo coming?" Instead of leaving, she leaned against the car. She might say she was fine, but she clearly wasn't ready to go home and read the waiting mail or listen to phone messages. With so many agencies involved in searching out Kasey's family, Nicki had no idea who would contact her or how.

"I should have it finished before Thanksgiving."

"It was a very nice gesture on your part to rebuild it."

"You said you missed it."

She blushed sweetly. "I'm sure I'm not the only one in town who does."

Before he could answer, a pickup pulled up next to them and Clay recognized Jesse behind the wheel. Rolling down the window, Jesse nodded to Nicki then sat silently staring at Clay for a long moment. Finally, he said, "I've been hearing that you're doing a good job for Bill Porter."

"Bill's a great guy to work for. He's almost as laid back as I am. How have you been? How are the girls?"

"We've been doing okay. A funny thing happened the day after you were there."

"Oh? What was that?"

"A woman named Clara Binter called me and asked if I needed a nanny." Jesse's gaze switched to Nicki. "I don't suppose you had anything to do with that?"

Nicki shook her head. "No."

Clay looked down at his boots and tried not to smile. "That's great. How's it working out?"

"So-so. Other funny things have been happening around the place, too," Jesse continued. "My feed wagon had a flat tire that fixed itself overnight."

"That is odd," Clay agreed.

"Then a section of my south fence mysteriously got new wire strung, and two of my horses that were out in that pasture were reshod."

"Huh."

Nicki moved close to Clay's side. "It sounds as if someone was just trying to help you the way you've helped others in the past, Jesse."

Clay saw the muscles in his brother's jaw tighten. "It's appreciated. Maya tells me she's planning a big dinner for Thanksgiving. Are you going to be around for that, Clay?"

"If that's okay with you."

"Far be it from me to upset Maya's plans."

Grinning in amusement, Clay replied, "A man could get hurt doing that."

"A man could get hurt doing a lot of foolish things. I understand you found the body out at the old trestle."

Clay's amusement drained away. "Yeah."

"Maya told me Tommy was with you. I hope you weren't putting hare-brained notions in his head about that place."

Even after all these years, Jesse couldn't stop being the critical older brother. "I told him Grandpa took us fishing there. Remember that?"

Jesse's eyes softened. "I remember."

Inside the car, Kasey began to fuss at being strapped into her seat. Nicki looked from Jesse to Clay. "I really should get going. Jesse was there something you needed?"

He opened his door and got out. "I was in town picking up some feed. One of the guys at the feed store said folks over in the next county found some stuff the tornado dropped in one of their corn fields and they brought it in yesterday. I thought I'd check the lost and found again for Marie's ring."

Nicki laid a hand on his arm. "I hope you find it."

"Not much chance of that, but it doesn't hurt to look." He tipped his hat to her and walked away.

As he opened the door to the church, Avery came dashing out. The teenager skidded to a halt and stared at Jesse, a startled expression on her face. A bright blush bloomed in her cheeks. She ducked her head and hurried away without speaking to any of them.

When Jesse entered the building, Nicki said, "I wonder what's wrong with Avery?"

"I think she's got a crush on my brother."

"You could be right. His situation is sad enough to tug at any woman's heartstrings."

Clay transferred attention back to Nicki. He couldn't imagine what Jesse had gone through. He couldn't imagine what it would be like to lose the woman he loved.

Nicki watched the turmoil of emotions play across Clay's face. She wanted to know what he was thinking, what he was feeling. The warmth of his regard brought a rush of pleasure that sent her heart somersaulting. All of the sudden, she didn't want to leave.

"When did you find the time to do all those things for your brother?"

He shrugged. "Mostly at night or very early in the

morning. It's been tough sneaking around. I was afraid one of his neighbors would call the cops on me. You should try shoeing a horse by the headlights of a truck. It ain't easy."

"It was a wonderful thing to do."

"I could see he was falling behind with the ranch work. I did a few odd chores. It was nothing."

But to Nicki's eyes, it was something special. It proved just how much the boy she used to know had matured. "I've changed my mind, Clay. Would you please drive me home?"

He looked mildly surprised. "Sure."

They were both silent on the short drive. When they reached her apartment, Nicki got out and waited while he freed Kasey from the backseat.

Clay hefted the little girl high into the air and settled her on his neck for a piggyback ride. "Better hold tight, sugar. We're going for a gallop while Mommy gets the mail."

With Clay keeping Kasey occupied, Nicki had a few moments to compose herself before opening her mailbox at the curb. As she was gathering her courage, Lori Martin came out of her apartment intent on the same task. "Hey, Nicki, any word?"

"Not yet." Taking a deep breath, Nicki opened her box. She sighed with relief when she found only a grocery store ad and her electric bill.

One more day without a letter from child services

telling her she'd have to turn Kasey over to her real family was one more day to rejoice.

Lori rubbed Nicki's shoulder. "I've been praying for you both."

"Thanks." It was good to know so many people cared.

Lori glanced to where Clay was playing with Kasey. "Jesse's brother seems to have a way with kids."

"Yes, he does."

"It must run in the family. Jesse was so good with his girls when they were in the hospital. I'll never forget the look on his face the day he came to visit them after his wife died. It broke my heart."

She blushed slightly as she looked at Nicki. "You know what I mean. Everyone in the unit felt sorry for him."

"I know what you mean."

Gesturing over her shoulder with her thumb, Lori said, "I've got to run. I'm working an extra shift tonight. See you later, Nicki."

As Lori left, Clay came trotting back and stopped beside her. Kasey, her blond hair in disarray and her cheeks glowing pink, had a big smile on her face and a death grip on Clay's head.

"Anything?" he asked.

Nicki held up the letters in her hand. "I never thought I'd be so happy to see my utility bill."

"That's just because you haven't opened it yet."

"True."

"I've been meaning to ask you something."

"Okay." She waited, wondering why he suddenly seemed nervous.

He cleared his throat. "I wanted to invite you, Kasey and your mother, of course, to the ranch for Thanksgiving. That is, if you don't already have plans of your own. I understand if you do, but I hope you don't."

"That's very sweet, but Thanksgiving is a day for you and your family."

"It's a day to give thanks. For family, for good food and especially for good friends. You'd better say yes. Maya is expecting you."

"I'll think about it."

He nodded toward her door. "Time to check the message machine."

"Do I have to?"

"Yes."

Heaving a sigh, she walked to the house and unlocked the door. She held it open as he went inside being careful to duck under the doorway so Kasey wouldn't bump her head.

Inside, Nicki immediately saw the light flashing on her answering machine. One message.

Turning away from the sight, she fixed her sights on Clay. "Can't we just get in my car and drive away? I've never been to Canada. We could go visit your friend Sadie."

Sadness filled his eyes. "You don't mean that, Nicki."

She did—if only for an instant. Her shoulders slumped. "No. I don't mean it. It was a foolish and cowardly thought."

Realizing what she'd just said, she clapped a hand to her mouth. "Oh, Clay, I'm so sorry. I didn't mean to imply—"

"That I was foolish and cowardly to run out on everyone here. That's not exactly news to me, Nicki. I figured that out about seven years too late."

Stepping close to him, she laid her palm over his heart. "You were wise and brave to return. It's not our mistakes that define us, Clay, it's what we do about them."

Kasey, having grown bored with her mount's inactivity, pounded on Clay's head. "Go, 'orsey man, go."

His gaze remained locked with Nicki's. "'Orsey man wants to stay right where he is."

"I want you to stay, too." Nicki whispered and bit her lip as she looked into his eyes knowing full well that she was laying her heart bare for him to see.

The joy that sprang to his face nearly took her breath away, but as suddenly as it appeared, it faded. "I've got nothing to offer you, Nicki. I've been a drifter most of my life. I'm not father or husband material."

"I disagree and so does Kasey."

Nicki could sense how much he wanted to believe

her. There was so much that needed to be said between them. She would have to tell him now, before their relationship went any further, that they would never have children of their own. Would it make a difference to him?

Gathering her courage, she said, "I'm going to put Kasey down for her nap and then there are some things I need to tell you."

"Okaaay." He lowered the child to the floor.

She took her foster daughter by the hand, walked to the answering machine and pressed play.

The message was from another teacher asking about her lesson plan. Relief pumped through Nicki's body, making her knees wobbly. She looked to Clay and saw the same emotion mirrored in his eyes.

"Would you like to stay for supper?" She wanted him to say yes.

It took several long seconds before he answered. She held her breath afraid he'd refuse. Finally, he nodded. "I'd like that."

She relaxed. "Good."

After getting her Kasey settled for her usual rest period, Nicki closed her bedroom door softly and braced herself to finish her conversation with Clay without interruptions.

He was sitting on the sofa looking as nervous as he had the night he'd shown up to take her to the prom. The memory softened her heart. She couldn't be mistaken about his feelings. He did care about her.

He rose to his feet. She crossed the room to stand in front of him. "There's a reason I started fostering babies. When I was in college, I became ill and had to have surgery. There were complications. Afterward, the doctors told me I'd never bear children."

"Nicki, I'm so sorry."

"I thought you should know."

"That doesn't change how I feel about you. I care for you so much. Both you and Kasey."

It was so hard to keep her practical thoughts in order when all she wanted was to be held in his arms, to feel his love surrounding her. "I care about you, too, Clay, but before we get more involved with each other, I have to know that you aren't going to pick up and leave one day."

"I won't. Not as long as you want me here."

"I'm not asking for a life-long commitment now, Clay. I'm only asking for a chance to see if these feelings we have are the real deal."

He smiled at her softly. "They must be because I've been thinking about doing this since the first day I got back in town."

He bent his head and kissed her. The gentle brush of his lips against hers filled her with longing and excitement. She circled his neck with her arms as he pulled her close.

When he finally lifted his head, she pressed her cheek against his chest. "I'm so glad God brought you back into my life."

The sound of the front door opening startled both of them. Clay stepped away from her. Nicki turned to see her mother come rushing in. Clearly upset, Glenis didn't seem to notice Nicki wasn't alone. "You'll never believe what's happened. This is just terrible. How could I have been so misled?"

"Mom, what's wrong?" Nicki left Clay's side.

Pacing the room, Glenis dragged her fingers through her disheveled hair. "That electrical contractor I hired has taken the building committee's money and skipped town. What's more, he's stolen money from a dozen other people, and it's all my fault. What are we going to do?"

Chapter Fourteen

"Calm down, Mom." Clay could hear the deep concern in Nicki's voice.

Glenis didn't stop her pacing. "I can't calm down. I just came from the bank. The man forged my signature and emptied the account. Of course, I knew it had to be some kind of mistake, so I went to the motel where he was staying, but he'd already checked out."

She paused as she caught sight of Clay. She glanced from him to Nicki with a deep scowl on her face. "I'm sorry. I didn't know you had company."

"Have you called the police?" Clay asked.

"Not yet," she admitted.

He pulled out his cell phone. "They may be able to find him before he gets too far."

She ignored his comment and turned to Nicki. "What am I going to tell the committee members?

Everyone was counting on getting the building finished by Christmas. We needed that money. If we can't get it back, I'll never be able to hold up my head again."

Nicki patted her mother's hand. "Clay's right. Let's see what Colt Ridgeway says before we do anything else."

Standing by the fireplace, Clay waited while Glenis spoke to the police. When she hung up, she dropped her head in her hands. "Colt is running a background check on the name I gave him, but he isn't hopeful that we'll get the money back. He wants me to come down and give a statement. How am I going to face Reverend Garrison, the mayor, the town council?"

Nicki slipped an arm around her mother. "Michael will understand, Mom. I'll drive you to the police station. You're too upset to get behind the wheel. Give me a few minutes to get Kasey up."

"I can drive her," Clay offered.

"Would you?" Nicki sent him a grateful look.

"Sure."

"Thank you. Mom, Clay's going to drive you to the station. I'll get a sitter to come stay with Kasey, and I'll meet you there."

To Clay's surprise, her mother agreed without protest.

As he drove her car downtown, Glenis sat silently

in the passenger's seat. He searched for the words to reassure her that things would turn out all right, but realizing that might not be the case, he kept quiet. It didn't take long to reach their destination.

Pulling into the parking lot, Clay stopped near the building entrance and turned off the engine. Glenis made no move to get out. After a long moment, she looked in his direction. "Nicki is terrified she's going to lose Kasey."

He wasn't expecting a change of topic. "I know she is."

"I warned her not to get too attached to the child."

"Nicki has a generous, giving nature, Mrs. Appleton. I don't think she could remain unattached to any child let alone one as adorable as Kasey."

"What are you really doing here, Clay?"

He frowned. "I'm not sure what you mean?"

"You broke my daughter's heart once before. I knew the minute I saw you back in High Plains that you'd do it again."

"Mrs. Appleton, I never had any intention of hurting Nicki. I'd do anything for her."

"I think you've done enough. Why can't you leave her alone?"

Grasping the top of the steering wheel with both hands, Clay bowed his head. Would Nicki be better off without him?

He'd been sure of that once, but he didn't believe

it now. Glenis, on the other hand, apparently saw things differently.

He said, "I care deeply for Nicki. She's capable of making up her own mind about our relationship, Mrs. Appleton. If she wants me in her life, that's where I'll be."

Clay pushed open the door and got out. Glenis did the same and rounded the hood to stand in front of him. She held out her hands for the keys and he dropped them into her palm.

Curling her fingers closed, she said, "My daughter is reliving a teenage fantasy with you. It won't last. Besides, she deserves better than some poor cowhand. I know it, and so do you. If you really cared about her, you'd make her see it, too."

She turned on her heels and entered the building leaving Clay standing on the sidewalk.

Her words were an echo of his own fears. He couldn't dismiss them from his mind as he crossed Main Street to the place where he'd left his truck. The rusty hinges of the door creaked as he pulled it open. Sliding into the driver's seat that had been repaired with duct tape in more than one spot, he realized just how little he had to offer Nicki. His gaze was drawn to the partially finished gazebo in the park.

A pair of young boys were playing tag and chasing each other around the perimeter of it. He listened to their shouting and laughter with half an ear.

The incomplete gazebo seemed to mock Clay. He'd told himself he wanted to rebuild it for Nicki. Maybe the truth was he'd rebuilt it for himself. As a way to make amends for his past sins.

Who was he kidding? A few sheets of plywood and some two-by-fours wouldn't cover that cost.

Bowing his head, he prayed for guidance and tried to put his own needs and desires aside and listen to what God wanted from him.

He had no idea how long he'd been sitting in his truck when his cell phone rang. The sun was setting and the western sky was streaked with crimson.

Pulling his phone from his pocket, he saw it was Nicki. He answered it and asked, "What did the police say?"

"If I had a nickel for each time I've heard that question this week I'd be a rich woman." Her voice sounded exhausted.

"Sorry."

"Don't be. I was teasing. The guy is a con artist. He and his group have hit other towns like ours. We aren't likely to get the money back. It's so unfair and cruel. We've worked so hard to recover. I'm afraid this may break the town's spirit."

"It won't. We come from pioneer stock, remember?"

"I pray you're right," Nicki said. "I hope you'll forgive me, but I'm going to back out on my offer of supper. Mom is so upset. I can't leave her alone tonight."

"I understand. Family comes first."

"Thank you. Once she's gotten over the shock, we'll think of a way to raise the money again."

"That's the spirit."

"Will I see you tomorrow?" she asked softly.

Outside his window, the boys had started a shoving match. The smaller boy planted his hands on his hips and shouted, "I don't have to do what you say. You're not the boss of me!"

Karen Dewey's belligerent young face sprang into Clay's mind followed by her father's grateful words. "If there is ever anything I can do for you, young man, all you have to do is ask."

Had Dewey mean it? Would he remember making the offer? Clay wasn't asking anything for himself. He wanted to help Nicki and the people of High Plains hang on to an important part of their heritage.

It wasn't the kind of request Clay could make over the phone. He'd need to see the man face-to-face, in case it took some convincing. Clay knew Dewey's company had its headquarters in Dallas, but he also knew the man traveled all over the world.

"Clay, are you there?" Nicki's voice snapped him out of his musing.

"I'm here."

"I asked if I'd see you tomorrow?"

"I'm not sure."

"Oh—okay."

He wanted to ease the disappointment in her words but he had no idea how long it might take him to gain a meeting with Dewey. "I'll call you soon, Nicki."

His plan was a long shot scheme at best. Clay didn't want to get her hopes up. She already had too many burdens on her shoulders. Besides, if he failed miserably, he'd rather she didn't know.

If he succeeded, he wanted to be there to see the delight in her eyes when he gave her the news in person.

The interior of the meeting hall sounded like a nest of angry hornets when Nicki and her mother entered it Saturday afternoon. As soon as they stepped through the door a crowd of volunteers surrounded them. Questions flew at them like buckshot.

"Is it true?"

"Is the money really gone?"

"What are the police doing?"

Nicki held up her hands for silence. "Yes, it's true. The money is gone. We aren't certain that we'll be able to recover any of it, but the police are working on that."

Allen, his face red with pent-up emotion, folded his arms tightly over his chest. "Glenis, I thought you checked this guy out? You told us his references were good. It's not just this project that's dead in the water. My brother lost a bundle. It will be months before he can get his family moved back into their home."

"The same thing happened to my uncle," someone else added.

Nicki understood their frustration and their anger. She wished Clay were here. She could use his moral support.

Glenis kept her chin up, and Nicki was proud of her. "The company I thought I was checking out is a real company. That's why the references were good. This man simply wasn't who he pretended to be."

"You should have thought of that."

Michael, who had entered the building in time to hear the last comment, crossed the room to stand at Nicki's side. "The man is a slick crook who's gotten away with schemes like this numerous times. No one is to blame except that man and his gang."

Michael had to raise his voice to be heard over the growing buzz of talk. "We can still go ahead with this project. Allen, where do we stand on materials?"

Happy to turn the spotlight over to the minister, Nicki's mother retreated to stand by the wall. Her gaze was drawn again and again to the door. Where was Clay? Why wasn't he here?

The story had spread quicker than one of the Flint Hill's grass fires. Surely Clay had to know the townspeople would rake her and her mother over the coals when they met today.

Nicki tried to stem the rising disappointment she felt, but it ate away at her. She needed him, but he wasn't here. Again.

Allen consulted a clipboard another volunteer handed him. "We've got enough wood to finish the stage and the exterior siding today. We have enough sheetrock to cover the north and east walls, but we simply can't put it up until the electrical goes in."

"Why not?" Glenis asked. "We can have the wiring put in later."

Allen shook his head. "After the ductwork and electrical conduits go in they still have to be inspected. Any inspector worth his salt will need to see all the wiring. He can make us pull down any sheetrock we've put up to expose the wiring behind it so we need the wiring done first. I'm sorry. We're at a standstill."

Stepping up to address the group, the mayor said, "We're going to finish what we can today. When that's done, let's all think about how we can raise the money to complete this building. We did it once, we can do it again."

"But not in time for Founders' Day," someone added bitterly from the rear.

Glenis's brave face finally crumpled.

As the disgruntled group split up to finish what they

could, Nicki saw Mayor Dawson lay a comforting hand on Glenis's shoulder. "We'll get through this."

Glenis, the mayor and several members of the town council moved into the kitchen area for a private meeting.

Maya came over to Nicki. She had been one of the few silent ones in the crowd. Smiling encouragingly, she asked, "How are you doing?"

"I feel terrible for my mother. She's having a hard time holding it together. She has poured her heart and soul into this project from the very beginning. This place meant so much to my father. I think rebuilding it is her way of expressing her love for him even though he's gone."

"The idea that someone is unscrupulous enough to take advantage of our trust after all we've been through is almost unbelievable. I hope the police nail him," Maya added with vengeance.

"I agree."

Once again Nicki glanced toward the door. Maya noticed. "Are you expecting someone else?"

"I thought Clay would be here."

Maya tipped her head. "I haven't seen him. Perhaps he's just running late."

Maybe, but why didn't Nicki think that was the case? He said he'd call, but he hadn't. Not yesterday, not today.

Maybe he'd changed his mind about continuing

their relationship. Perhaps he couldn't accept that he'd never have sons and daughters of his own if he decided to share his life with her.

"Has Clay asked you to join our family for Thanksgiving dinner?" Maya asked.

"Yes, he did."

"And what was your answer?"

Perhaps Clay was sorry now that he'd extended the invitation. Nicki hedged. "I said I'd think about it."

"And have you?"

"I'm not sure what my mother has planned."

"Here she comes. Let's ask her."

Maya, in her friendly, fearless manner, met Glenis halfway across the room. Nicki followed.

"Mrs. Appleton, I'd like to extend an invitation to you and your daughter to join my family for Thanksgiving dinner. I won't take no for an answer."

"That's very kind of you, Mrs. Garrison," Glenis replied in a low, shaky voice that Nicki barely recognized.

She glanced at Nicki and said, "I'm afraid I won't be able accept. I'm leaving Monday evening. I'm going to St. Louis to spend the week with my sister."

It was the first Nicki had heard of the plan, but she couldn't blame her mother for wanting to leave town for a little while.

"That's too bad," Maya said, but quickly turned to Nicki. "Does this mean you'll be free that day?"

"Looks like it."

"Then we can expect you and Kasey?"

Not wanting to sound ungracious, Nicki agreed. "Sure."

"Great. Tommy and Layla love playing with Kasey, and I know Jesse and Clay will both be thrilled you can join us."

Nicki prayed that was true. Either way, Maya was a good friend, and Nicki knew she'd been looking forward to the day since Clay's return. Nicki would go for her sake.

It wasn't until after Nicki returned home that evening that the call from Clay finally came. When she heard his voice, it was as if a hundred-pound weight had been lifted from her. Relief and happiness made her giddy.

She curled into the chair in her living room with the phone pressed to her ear. "Hey, 'orsey man. I was wondering what had happened to you."

"The truth is I had to make a quick trip out of town."

"You, too, huh? First the contractor, then my mother and now my daughter's new favorite horsey."

"Have you sent the law after me, too?"

"Not yet, but I was thinking about it." And about how much she missed and wanted him with her.

"I'll be back Monday evening."

Two long days away. "Promise?"

"I do, and I'm bringing you a gift."

"What is it?" she demanded. Not that she cared. Seeing him again was all that mattered.

"I'm not telling, but you're going to like it. I've missed you, Nicki…and Kasey. I had no idea how much until I heard your voice." His words simmered with a low intensity that made her shiver in delight.

"I've missed you, too. Hurry home."

"Wild horses couldn't keep me away. Not even a mule named Sadie."

After he hung up, Nicki stayed in the chair with her arms crossed over her middle. Excitement hummed in her veins. She didn't know if she wanted to burst into song or waltz around the room or both. Clay was coming home to her. All her worry had been for nothing.

Thank You, Lord. Thank You for bringing this wonderful man into my life.

The following days passed slowly. Anticipation made the time drag. But no matter what she was doing to fill the hours, cleaning the house, raking leaves in the yard or watching her preschool class make Thanksgiving decorations, she found herself humming and smiling. Clay would be back soon.

When she got home after school on Monday, the delicious aroma of the stew that had been simmering all day in her slow cooker filled the apartment. Hopefully, it would help convince Clay to stay for supper.

She quickly gave the house a run-through with her

duster and picked up Kasey's toys. The doorbell rang as she was putting a set of blocks away. After pausing to take a peek at her hair and face in the mirror, she hurried to the front door and pulled it open.

It wasn't Clay.

A woman in a dark suit holding a leather brief-case stood unsmiling on the stoop. Two sheriff's officers flanked her. The woman asked, "Are you Miss Nicki Appleton?"

Nicki's happiness died a quick death. It was replaced by heart-pounding fear. "Yes, I am."

The woman withdrew a thick folded document from her case and extended it. "I'm Pauline Brock of the Kansas City Child Services Office. This is a court order requiring you to immediately surrender Katherine Cassidy to the custody of Wilma Cassidy, the child's maternal great-aunt."

Chapter Fifteen

Clay bounded up the steps of Nicki's apartment with eager anticipation. The drive from Dallas had been a long one. He was later than he thought he would be, but it didn't matter now.

He couldn't wait to see her, couldn't wait to see her happiness when he gave her the news.

He rapped on her door knowing he had a foolish grin on his face. He didn't care. What man didn't smile like a fool when he was about to give the girl of his dreams a present?

When the door opened, he found himself face-to-face with Nicki's mother. Her cold appraisal took his smile down a couple of notches.

Pulling of his hat, he nodded to her. "Hello, Mrs. Appleton, is Nicki at home?"

"She is, but she isn't seeing anyone," she replied sharply.

"She's expecting me."

"I'm sure you're the last person she wants to see at this moment. I think you should leave."

That killed his smile altogether. "What's wrong?"

"Child services took Kasey away an hour ago."

"What? Why would they do that?" Even as the question spilled from his mouth, he knew the answer. "They located her family."

"Yes. The child has a maternal great-aunt in Kansas City who intends to raise her."

"But Nicki has already started the adoption process. Can't she fight this?"

"If the adoption had been finalized, perhaps, but not now. A few more weeks is all it would have taken, but your discovery robbed her of that time."

A sick knot formed in the pit of his stomach. He had destroyed his own family. Now, he'd destroyed Nicki's chance to keep the child she loved. Why had God let this happen?

"Will Nicki be able to see Kasey again? I mean, can't she at least visit her?"

"Not without her guardian's permission. The social worker who came today told Nicki that the great-aunt believes a clean break would be best for the everyone. She thinks lingering goodbyes and visits would only confuse the child."

"It's not right."

"It's the way it is." For the first time, he saw a crack in Glenis's stoic face. Looking as she might break down, she closed her eyes and took several quick breaths.

Clay put his hand on the door. "I need to see Nicki."

Glenis regained her composure but didn't budge. "She's crying her eyes out in her bedroom. Go away, Clay. Go back to where ever you came from. Leave my daughter to grieve in peace."

He took a step backward, his mind reeling with regret and confusion. "I never meant to hurt her. I love Nicki."

"The sad thing is—I believe you. Please go."

Maybe she was right. Maybe he should give Nicki a chance to grieve in private. Knowing what she must be going through put a huge ache in his chest. He longed to hold her and offer what comfort he could. It was unbearable to think they would never see Kasey again.

He withdrew the envelope from his pocket. It was his big news. News that seemed very small compared to the heartbreak that had occurred today.

He extended the letter to Mrs. Appleton. "I want you and Nicki to have this."

She hesitated, then accepted it.

Clay put his hat on. "Please tell Nicki...that I'm sorry."

Turning around, he walked slowly back to his

truck. As he slid behind the steering wheel, he suddenly realized where he needed to go.

A few minutes later, he entered the hushed silence of the church sanctuary. The thick maroon carpet in the aisle muffled his footsteps as he walked forward. Stopping a few pews from the front, he sat down and lifted his gaze to the wooden cross before him.

Tears pricked his eyes. "I'm here, Jesus. I came home because I believed that was what You wanted. Was it? Was I wrong? I'm trying to understand. I've hurt so many people that I love. How can I make it right?"

Clasping his hands together, he bowed his head. "Lord, send Your comfort to Nicki and to Kasey. They must both feel lost and scared. I know I do."

Wiping his eyes on his shirtsleeve, he looked up. "Take care of them. Please."

Clay sat for a while longer, absorbing the peace and serenity of church. A sudden sound made him look over to see Reverend Michael Garrison entering through a side door. Michael paused for a second when he caught sight of Clay, then approached. "I'm sorry if I disturbed you."

"Don't be. It's your house."

"It's His house, so you are welcome to stay as long as you need. Is there something that I can do for you?"

"Tell me how I know what He wants from me."

Michael took a seat beside Clay. "I think Jesus

laid that out pretty well. We are to love God with all our heart and minds and to love our neighbor as ourselves."

How could Clay love the people who'd destroyed Nicki's dreams? "In theory that sounds pretty simple. In reality, it ain't so easy."

Michael smiled. "So I've noticed."

"Kasey was taken away from Nicki today."

"I just heard. Emma Barnet called me. She's a friend of Nicki's and our local social worker. She's very upset at the way the whole thing was handled. I'm on my way over to Nicki's now."

"They don't want Nicki to even visit Kasey. It's not right. That little girl has lost two mothers now."

"We must pray that Miss Cassidy has a change of heart. Mrs. Barnet has suggested Nicki petition the court for visitation rights. Both Emma and I will testify on Nicki's behalf.

"How long will that take?"

Michael shook his head sadly. "I have no idea."

"Thank you for trying to help."

Rising, Michael nodded. "Clay, the way we know what He wants from us is to examine our hearts. The answer is there if we aren't afraid to look."

As Michael walked away, the meaning of his words sank in. Clay realized he *had* been afraid to look inside his own heart. Deep down he believed he didn't deserve the love of his family or Nicki's love.

He turned and called out, "Reverend Garrison, do you know the name of Kasey's new guardian or where she lives?"

"All I know is that her last name is Cassidy and that she lives in Kansas City."

It wasn't much, but it was a start. Clay rose to his feet and walked toward Michael. "When you see Nicki, please tell her that I'm thinking of her and that I'm praying for her."

Michael gave him a knowing smile. "I think you should tell yourself. After all, you're in love with the woman."

Momentarily taken aback, Clay looked at Michael in surprise. "Is it that obvious?"

"Yes."

"I do love her. And I intend to tell her, but I've got something I have to do first in Kansas City."

Michael's face grew sober. "You aren't going to do something foolish, are you?"

Clay just smiled. "I've been doing foolish things all my life. Why change now?"

Nicki sat up on the side of her bed and wiped away the last of her tears. Her whole body ached with loss, but she was done crying. She had to face the fact that she would never see Kasey again. All she could do now was pray that her little girl would have a happy, loving home.

Rising, Nicki opened her bedroom door and walked down the hall toward the bathroom. On the way, she passed the closed door of Kasey's room. Soon, she would have to put away the clothes, the bedding, even the toys that Kasey loved. But not now. Not today.

After splashing water on her face and dragging a comb through her hair, Nicki walked into the living room. Her mother was sitting on the sofa staring out the window. Her arms were folded tightly across her middle as if holding in the pain.

"Are you okay, Mom?"

Glenis looked at her. "I should be asking you that. Never mind, we both know the answer. No, we are not okay."

Sinking onto the couch, Nicki welcomed the comfort of her mother's embrace. They leaned against each other, drawing strength from one another.

Glenis smoothed back Nicki's hair and tipped her chin up to examine her face. "I'm so sorry."

"I love her so much. I miss her already." Nicki didn't think she had any tears left, but they began to flow unchecked.

"Hush, baby." Glenis rocked her back and forth as if Nicki were a child again.

"What am I going to do, Mama?"

"You're going to grieve, darling."

"I wish Daddy were here."

"I wish that, too."

They sat together in silence for a long time. Finally, Nicki found the strength to pull away. "I have to stop crying. Clay will be here soon. I don't want him to see me like this. He'll blame himself."

Sighing deeply, Glenis said, "Clay has already been here. Reverend Garrison stopped by, as well."

"Why didn't you tell me Clay was here?"

"You were so upset. I thought it was best not to disturb you."

Nicki shot to her feet. "Mom, how could you do that? I know you didn't like Clay much when we were in school together."

"He was always so irresponsible. He was a bad influence on you."

"He's changed. Besides, we're not school kids anymore. We're adults. Clay and I belong together. I love him the way you loved Dad. You're going to have to accept that."

"Nicki, you could do so much better for yourself."

"How could I do better than to love a man with all my heart and soul?"

A look of defeat settled over her mother's features. "I guess I shouldn't be surprised. You always did take after your father. He was never the most practical man in the world."

"Dad loved God, and he loved you. What else does a man need?"

"Yes, that's exactly what he would have said."

Nicki moved to pick up the phone. "I have to call Clay. I know he must be as upset as I am."

She punched in his number but after several rings it went to voice mail. Disappointed, she left a brief message asking him to call, then returned to sit beside her mother.

Glenis pulled an envelope from her purse beside the couch and handed it to Nicki. "Clay wanted you to have this."

Nicki opened it and pulled out a letter. As she unfolded it, a slip of paper fluttered to the floor. She read the letter once and then read it again unable to believe what she was seeing. She pressed a hand to her heart as it swelled with pride and love.

Clay had done this for her, for all of High Plains. She handed the note to her mother. "It's from a man named Dewey. He owns a hotel-construction business in Dallas. He's sending a crew of electricians to finish the wiring on the Old Town Hall and any other homes in town that need work. They'll be here Friday. Plus, he's included a check for double the amount of money that was stolen from us as a personal favor to Clay. He says Clay saved his daughter's life."

Picking up the check, Nicki handed it to her mother. "I think this proves Clay isn't an irresponsible man."

Glenis pressed her fingers to her throat. "Oh, dear. I hope you can forgive me."

"Forgive you for what?"

"I told him you blamed him for losing Kasey."

Nicki could only stare at her mother in shock. "Why would you do that?"

"Because I thought it would be best for you if he left."

"He won't leave. Not now. Not when he knows I need him."

"That's just it. Reverend Garrison told me Clay has gone. He's on his way to Kansas City, and Michael is worried he's going to do something rash."

Chapter Sixteen

❧

Clay rang the doorbell of a small brick home located in an older section of Kansas City. Looking around, he saw a neighborhood slipping past its prime. The sidewalks were cracked and buckled. The chocolate-brown trim of the house in front of Clay was badly in need of painting, as were several of the neighboring buildings.

The surrounding streets were quiet, but then it was only nine o'clock on Thanksgiving morning.

The Kansas City phone book listed fourteen Cassidys. This was the twelfth address he'd visited in the last two days.

As he waited for someone to answer the bell, he prayed this was the right house, and that he'd be able to convince a total stranger that Kasey and Nicki belonged together.

Please, Lord, don't let me mess this up.

The door opened. A weary looking white-haired woman in a blue print housedress stood on the other side of the screen door. She looked at him with mild suspicion. "Yes, may I help you?"

Clay pulled off his cowboy hat. "Are you Miss Cassidy?"

"Yes."

"My name is Clay Logan, ma'am. Do you have a great niece by the name of Katherine?"

Suddenly, Kasey appeared beside the woman. Her little face lit up. "Hi! Hi, 'orsey man. Go ride. Please?"

Looking from the child to Clay, the elderly woman smiled. "It seems that she recognizes you."

The woman pushed open the screen, and Kasey tumbled out into Clay's waiting arms. He hugged her tightly. Grinning, she patted his face between her hands. "'Orsey man. Love you."

Rising, with the little girl in his arms, he smiled at her. "Hey, sugar, how you doing? I've been missing you."

Peering over Clay's shoulder, Kasey frowned. "Where Ni Ni?"

"Nicki's at home, honey."

Looking confused, Kasey said, "Me go home. Me go wif Mommy Ni Ni."

Clay transferred his gaze to Miss Cassidy. "That's what I'd like to talk to your aunt about."

Miss Cassidy folded her arms over her chest and

pressed her lips tightly together. Clay watched the indecision play across her face. Finally, she nodded and led the way inside.

He let out a long breath of relief.

Following the woman to her tiny living room, he took a seat on her blue floral sofa. A few of Kasey's toys were scattered about, the room itself was clean and tidy if overcrowded with furniture and knickknacks.

His eyes were drawn to the dozens of pictures lined up on the mantel and covering the wood paneling of the walls.

He tried to set Kasey down, but she squawked in protest and held on to his neck. Patting her back to reassure her, he allowed her to stay on his lap and gave her his cowboy hat to play with. She giggled and immediately began her favorite game of peek-a-boo covering her head with the hat and then lifting it up to grin at him.

Taking a seat opposite them in a padded rocker, Miss Cassidy folded her hands in front of her. They were gnarled and work-worn and bare of any jewelry. "Katherine has been asking for Ni Ni all the time."

"Ni Ni is her name for Nicki Appleton. Nicki has been Kasey's…I'm sorry…Katherine's foster mother since July. Allow me to offer my condolences on the death of your niece."

"Thank you."

Clay nodded toward a framed portrait of a young woman with dark brown hair and hazel eyes on the mantel. Clay saw only a slight resemblance to the child he held. "Is that Dana?"

"Yes. She was my brother's only child. He was nearly fifteen years younger than I. We were never very close until his wife became ill. Dana's mother died of cancer five years ago. My brother died of a heart attack a year later. I often thought it more the case of a broken heart. He missed her terribly." Miss Cassidy sat quietly staring at the portrait.

Clay saw the sorrow deeply etched on her face. "What was Dana like?"

Glancing back to him, Miss Cassidy smiled softly. "She was a dreamer, always flitting from one job to another, from one man to another. After her father died, she ran away with some young man, but they didn't stay together. She wrote a few times that first year, but I never heard from her after that. I didn't even know that she'd had a child."

"That's why you didn't come forward."

"I heard about the toddler who was found after the tornado, of course. It was in the news for weeks, but I never connected that child to Dana. The police believe she was on her way here when she was killed. I'd like to think that. I'd like to think she had straightened out her life and wanted me to meet her daughter."

Clay chose his next words carefully. "Ms. Cassidy,

I can't imagine how difficult this has been for you, but Nicki Appleton is...someone very dear to me."

Kasey stopped playing and looked around. "Ni Ni?"

Clay ruffled her hair. "Nicki loves this little girl with all her heart. She was planning to adopt her. I came here today to ask if you would allow Nicki to visit Katherine."

"One hears such terrible things about foster care these days. When they told me Dana had a daughter who'd been in foster care for all those months, I couldn't bear the thought."

"She was in a loving home from the minute she was released from the hospital."

"But she wasn't with family."

How could he make her understand that that was exactly where Kasey had been? His gaze was once again drawn to the photos on the mantel. The answer, he realized, was right in front of his eyes.

Clay pulled his phone from his pocket. It took him a second but he finally accessed the video he'd made at the day care the week before.

Setting Kasey aside, Clay rose and handed the phone to Miss Cassidy. "Love is what makes a family. This is the woman who loves your great niece. Please, let her stay in this little girl's life. It will mean the world to both of them."

As the recording played, Clay watched emotions

cross the elderly woman's face. He could hear Nicki's voice and the sound of Kasey's happy greeting. He didn't need to see it, he'd memorized the loving look on Nicki's face as she held and rocked the child of her heart.

"Me see." Kasey, tossing his hat aside, hurried to her aunt's side and climbed into her lap. She pulled the phone from Miss Cassidy's hands.

Grinning up at the adults, Kasey said, "My mommy. My Ni Ni."

She brought the phone to her lips and planted a kiss on the screen.

Parking her car in front of Jesse's house, Nicki wished she hadn't given in to Maya's pleading at church. She'd never felt less like celebrating Thanksgiving in her life. Nor did she feel like spending it alone. This was the lesser of the two evils. Besides, there was still a slim chance that Clay would show up.

Tommy and Layla were taking advantage of the beautiful weather and were playing with a soccer ball at the side of the house. Layla was laughing as she tried to steal the black and white ball from Tommy.

Was Kasey having a happy Thanksgiving with her great-aunt? Was she laughing her adorable giggle? Nicki tried to believe that she was.

Bracing herself, she put on what she hoped was

a less-than-sad face. Maya, too, had to be dealing with her share of disappointment after learning Clay wouldn't be there.

Where was he? Why hadn't he called?

The answers weren't in her car. Nicki opened the door and stepped out. She heard the front screen door slam and looked up expecting to see Maya or Jesse coming to greet her. Instead, she saw Clay grinning from ear to ear. In his arms, he held her Kasey.

Shrieking with joy, Nicki raced up the steps and pulled Kasey into a fierce hug. Smothering her cute baby face with kisses, Nicki thought her heart would burst with happiness. It felt so wonderful to hold her.

"Happy Thanksgiving," Clay said, smiling at her.

"How did you do this?" She looked at him in astonishment.

"I beat down a few dozen doors, then kidnapped her from a white-haired lady."

Nicki's eyes widened with shock. "You didn't?"

"No, but I had you for a second, didn't I?"

Slowly, Nicki became aware that they weren't alone. Clay's family had gathered around. Maya, with an enormous grin on her face, was holding hands with Greg while Jesse stood looking on from the doorway. Tommy was making faces while Layla was busy trying to punch the soccer ball out of his hands. Behind him, a small gray-haired woman Nicki didn't know was watching it all with interest.

Following Nicki's gaze, Clay said, "Nicki, this is Miss Wilma Cassidy, Katherine's great-aunt."

With a sinking sensation, Nicki realized Kasey wasn't back for good. She was only here for a visit. Her grip on the child tightened. Yet, if Miss Cassidy had allowed one visit, perhaps she could be convinced to allow more.

Nicki stepped toward the woman. "I can't thank you enough for bringing Katherine here today. I've missed her so much."

"Who's Katherine?" Tommy quipped.

Wilma tipped her head slightly as she regarded the boy. "That happens to be my great-niece's given name, but you can continue to call her Kasey. I think that's a name that fits her."

Layla finally managed to free the ball from Tommy's hands and took off with it. Shouting his ire, he ran after her.

Wilma smiled at the horseplay. "My brother used to drive me crazy when he was Layla's age. It wasn't until later that we became friends. Miss Appleton, Mr. Logan tells me that your intention was to adopt Kasey. I'd like to hear more about those plans."

Hope sprang up like a startled deer in Nicki's chest, robbing her of breath. Was it possible? Miss

Cassidy turned and walked to a pair of white whicker chairs at the end of the porch.

Nicki's gaze flew to Clay. The abiding love in his eyes gave her courage. She held out her hand, and he gripped it tightly. "Thank you."

"Go. Convince her that she and Kasey can both be a part of your family for as long as they live."

Clay watched Nicki and Kasey's great-aunt deep in conversation at the other end of the porch. Their smiling faces were turned toward Kasey playing near their feet, but occasionally, Nicki looked up to meet Clay's eyes and gift him with a beautiful smile that warmed his heart.

Layla came pounding up the steps, a serious pout on her face. "Tommy won't play with me. I'm gonna tell Mom!"

Shouting for her mother, she stormed into the house. Out beside the barn, Jesse, squatting on his heels, was deep in conversation with Tommy. When Tommy walked away, Jesse picked something up from the grass.

Nicki's laughter drew Clay's attention. He smiled at the radiant glow on her face. Kasey was demonstrating her dancing ability by gyrating wildly to a tune Miss Cassidy was humming for her.

"You did a good thing."

Clay glanced over his shoulder to find his brother

standing behind him. Jesse's praise meant more than he would ever know. "Thanks. I have to admit, I'm feeling a bit like Father Christmas."

"Don't let it go to your head."

"I'll try not to."

"Here." Jesse extended his hand. He held a small black glass horse. "One leg seems to be missing, but I'm amazed it isn't in worse shape. I must have walked past that clump of grass a hundred times since the storm. Guess I was meant to find it today. You should keep it. You always liked it."

"Thanks. This means a lot." Clay closed his fingers around one of his grandmother's treasures. The shadowbox might be gone, but he could build a new one and start a collection for Kasey and her children. That is—if he could convince Nicki to marry him.

"How's the job at the Rocking P going?" Jesse asked.

"I knew it was only temporary when I took it. I'm going to have to look for something else now that I'm not heading back to Canada. Any suggestions?"

Jesse rubbed a hand over his chin. "It wouldn't pay much more than the Rocking P, but you might consider working on the Circle-L, instead."

Clay looked at his brother in disbelief. "You're asking me to come to work with you. For real?"

"We could try it and see how it goes. No promises."

Deep emotions tightened Clay's throat. Maybe

someday he'd be able to redeem himself in Jesse's eyes. "Thanks. I'd really like that."

"Guess we should go in and give Maya's turkey a try. I've got to admit, I'm a little leery."

The smells of roast turkey, dressing and apple pie drifting out of the house were enough to make Clay's mouth water. "You're thinking of that meatloaf she used to make."

"Yeah. How did you know that?"

"The look on your face. Who could forget that disaster? Actually, she's grown into a pretty good cook."

"You're kidding, right?"

"No, her chili is awesome."

"Are you talking about me?" Maya, who had gone inside, reappeared holding one of the triplets.

"I'll take her," Jesse said, smiling softly at his daughter.

Maya handed her over. "It's wonderful having you both here."

Clay ruffled her hair. "If you're this excited now, what are you going to be like at Christmas?"

Her grin faded a little. "I hope it will be as happy a day as this one, but Greg and I have run into a problem with our plans for Tommy's adoption."

Jesse nodded toward the door. "I hear one of the other girls crying. Let's go inside."

In the living room, Jesse handed Brooke back to

Maya and picked up Madison. When he had her quiet, he turned to his sister. "I thought the adoption was going to be final in a few weeks."

"It should be, but there's been a snag with the paperwork. We wanted to give Tommy the news on Christmas Day, but it looks like it will be after the first of the year."

"Mom, something's burning," Layla announced from the kitchen doorway.

Maya pushed Brooke into Clay's arms and rushed to the kitchen. Jesse and Clay exchanged amused glances. Just then Nicki, with Kasey in her arms, came in followed by Miss Cassidy.

Nicki's gaze met Clay's. Her eyes were brimming with happiness. He gathered his courage and asked, "Nicki can I speak to you for a second?"

"Sure."

He caught her hand and led her back out onto the porch and around to the side of the house. Once there, his courage wavered.

"You'll never guess what?" Nicki began in an excited rush. She kissed Kasey's cheek and hugged her close. "Miss Cassidy has agreed to let me go ahead with Kasey's adoption. Her only stipulation is that she be allowed to visit frequently. Can you believe it?"

"That's great."

"Yes, it is. I'm so happy. But what did you want to tell me?"

"I wanted to tell you that I love you beyond all reason, Nicki Appleton, and I'll never be a whole man until I have you by my side forever. I want us to be a family. You and Kasey and me. Will you marry me?"

"Yes, oh, yes. This is the happiest day of my life." She threw one arm around his neck and hugged him tightly.

He gathered her and Kasey close. Nuzzling Nicki's hair, he whispered. "You are what I've been looking for all my life. I'm so glad the Lord led me back to you."

"I love you, Clay. I don't think I'll ever get tired of saying that." She cupped his cheek with her palm and kissed him with a tenderness that dispelled any doubts he may have had.

In that instant, Clay knew he had ended up exactly where God intended him to be. Home—with a family of his own.

The Saturday after Thanksgiving, Nicki drove into the church parking lot and got out of her car. Glancing across to the park, she saw Clay putting up the last panel of lattice on the gazebo. Her heart overflowed with love and gratitude for the man who'd returned so much to her and to her town.

The man she was going to marry. The thought sent bubbles of happiness zipping through her. They'd talked about a spring wedding but hadn't set a date yet.

She crossed the winter-brown grass to watch him work. As he nailed the final wall in place, she began clapping.

He turned around and saw her. The look of love that filled his eyes sent joy flooded into every fiber of her being.

He took a small bow. "Thank you, ma'am."

"It looks beautiful, Clay."

"Not as beautiful as you."

"Ah, what a sweet thing to say."

"I'm a sweet guy."

"I've heard that about you. Everyone in High Plains is singing your praises." She glanced over her shoulder at the Old Town Hall where a flurry of construction was underway thanks to the arrival of the crew from Dallas.

Clay stepped backward inside the pavilion and beckoned her by crooking one finger. "Come here, soon-to-be Mrs. Logan."

Managing a coy look, she shook her head. "I don't think so. I seem to remember that you made improper advances to me the last time we were inside a place just like this."

Crossing his arms, he leaned his shoulder against the frame of the opening. "All the more reason you should come here, now."

"And why's that?"

"Because I'd like to make some *proper* advances toward you."

"Well, why didn't you say so?" Sauntering up to him, she lifted her face for his kiss.

He didn't hesitate. He pulled her inside and proceeded to kiss her breathless. Drawing away at last, he smiled into her eyes. "Was that better than the last time?"

"It was good, but I think you need a little more practice."

He growled and jerked her close once more. The shrill ring of his phone interrupted them.

Releasing her, he pulled it from his pocket. "I think I liked it better before I had one of these."

Opening it, he said, "This better be important, Jesse, because your timing stinks."

Nicki chuckled, but as Clay's face grew sober so did her own. She listened to the terse conversation with growing concern. Then Clay said, "Nicki's right here. I'll ask her."

Holding his hand over the phone, Clay said, "Tommy is missing."

"What?"

"Maya took the kids out to the ranch to visit today. She was getting ready to leave but they can't find Tommy anywhere. They think he's run away. Jesse wants to know if you can come out to the ranch and watch the babies while he gets a search party together."

"Tell him absolutely. I'll be there as soon as I can."

Clay spoke into the phone again. "We're on our way."

He hung up and tucked the phone in his pocket, then he cupped her face between his hands and gave her a quick kiss. "Thanks, I knew you'd help."

"Of course. They're my family, too." Grabbing his hand, she pulled him toward the church and her waiting car.

"I'm afraid that boy is going **to give** Maya as much grief as I gave my folks."

As they hurried across the park, Nicki knew this was how it was meant to be. The two of them facing whatever challenges lay ahead, together—hand in hand—and trusting in God's loving grace to carry them through.

* * * * *

Dear Reader,

I hope you enjoyed *A Family for Thanksgiving* and all the stories in the AFTER THE STORM series. The old saying that truth is stranger than fiction certainly held true for me in writing this book.

Several weeks after I was invited to participate in this continuity by Steeple Hill in the summer of 2008, the town of Chapman, Kansas, was heavily damaged by a tornado. I attended high school in Chapman and it has always been a place dear to my heart. The damage to the community was extensive, but just as the town of High Plains struggled and succeeded in recovering, so are the residents of Chapman facing their heartache with faith in God and in each other.

No element of this story was taken from that tragedy. In fact, the basis for the series was laid out months before that tornado struck. However, I know that photos, news stories and eyewitness accounts of that event helped add realism to my own story.

Chapman's road to recovery has been long and it isn't over yet. The town will bear the scars of that storm for decades. But the people of Kansas are a resilient bunch. I have no doubt that their community will emerge stronger and more steadfast because of the trials they have borne. I wish them well and ask that you keep them in your prayers.

As always, I enjoy hearing from readers. You can contact me by mail at P.O. Box 16714, Wichita, Kansas 67216, or e-mail me at:
pat@patriciadavids.com.

Blessings,

Patricia Davids

QUESTIONS FOR DISCUSSION

1. Clay's renewal of faith occurred in a life-and-death struggle to save a child. Do you know someone whose faith was reborn from a life-changing event?

2. Clay sought answers to why God sent him back to High Plains. What answers do you seek from God in your own life?

3. Both Clay and Nicki recognize that their attraction in high school wasn't lasting love. What part of that relationship did they cling to and why?

4. Has your community or the community of someone you know been affected by a natural disaster? How did that impact your faith?

5. Nicki's mother did not approve of Clay. Have you, or someone you know, faced similar opposition to a romance? How did those feelings change the outcome for the couple? For the rest of the family?

6. What symbolism did water play in this story?

7. Clay and his brother achieved the start of a reconciliation in *A Family for Thanksgiving*. Have you had a falling-out with a family member? How has that changed your life?

8. Clay doubted that he would make a good father. If you have children, what doubts have you had about your ability to parent? How has your faith played a role in this?

9. What do you see as the real reason Clay wanted to rebuild the gazebo?

10. The loss of Tommy's dog in the storm is a heartache the little boy couldn't bear to face. Pets sometimes play an important role in our lives. Do you own a pet? Have you lost a pet you loved? If so, how did that impact your life?

11. What do you foresee for Clay and Nicki in their lives? What would you imagine them doing in five years? In ten year? In fifty years?

12. How has this story or this series changed your perception of Kansas?

13. Nicki couldn't have children of her own and was brave enough to foster babies in need. Do

you know people willing to open their homes and hearts to such children? What blessing has this added to their lives?

14. The Logan family engagement ring has never been found. What heirloom, if any, do you hope to pass on in your family?

15. The next book in the series is Clay's brother Jesse's story, *Jingle Bell Babies*. What do you think will happen between the brothers in that book?

Turn the page for a sneak preview of Jessie Logan's story, JINGLE BELL BABIES by Kathryn Springer, the conclusion to the heartwarming AFTER THE STORM miniseries available in December from Love Inspired.

Prologue

July 11, 1:15 p.m.

"One of the tornadoes that touched down in the area yesterday and struck the small town of High Plains was determined to be a level F3. Already the Red Cross, local law-enforcement agents and volunteers have banded together to begin cleanup—"

Jessie Logan reached out and stabbed his finger against the power button on the radio.

He didn't need a reporter to condense the past twenty-four hours into a neat little sound bite. Or try to describe the damage a second tornado had caused when it churned across the prairie and targeted the Circle-L.

Jessie had not only seen the devastation firsthand, he was standing in the middle of it.

The kitchen lay in shambles around him. The

twister had spared the outbuildings but clipped the side of the ranch house, taking out a section of the wall while leaving his mother's antique china cabinet in the corner of the room intact. Glass from the shattered window littered the floor, strewn among soggy tufts of insulation and chunks of sodden wallboard.

Jessie picked up a piece of wood and was about to pitch it into a growing pile of debris when he realized it was one of the legs from the kitchen table.

His fingers tightened around it, ignoring the splinters that bit into his skin.

Yesterday morning he'd sat at that table before going out to do his chores.

And yesterday afternoon...

A fresh wave of pain crashed over Jesse, bringing with it a series of images that made him wonder if he wasn't still caught in the throes of a nightmare. Except that his eyes weren't closed.

The crunch of tires against gravel momentarily broke through his turbulent thoughts. For a split-second, hope stirred inside his chest as he sent up a silent prayer that the car coming up the driveway would be a familiar one.

It was.

The hammer slipped out of Jessie's hand and grazed a crease in the hardwood floor as the High Plains squad car stopped in front of the house.

Cold Ridgeway's tall frame unfolded from the passenger side.

As the police chief approached, the stoic set of his jaw and the regret darkening his eyes told Jessie everything.

No. No. No.

"This is going to be hard for you to hear, Jesse." His friend's quiet words barely penetrated the rushing sound in Jessie's head. "Late this morning…homeowners found Marie's vehicle on their property…tree fell on the driver's side…"

Like a child, Jessie wanted to press his hands against his ears and shut out the truth.

Where are You, God? Are You even listening? How much more do You think one man can take?

The silent cry burst out of a place deep inside him. Hadn't he gone through enough?

"Marie must have been trying to outrun the tornado," Colt continued softly. "I'm so sorry for your loss, Jessie. Sorry for you…and your girls."

Jessie couldn't answer. Couldn't tell Colt the truth. Not yet. That his wife hadn't been trying to outrun the tornado—she'd been running away. From him.

When the driving rain had forced him to abandon his chores the day before, he'd found Marie's note on the kitchen table. Next to it, the simple gold wedding band and diamond engagement ring he'd given to her the night he'd proposed.

An heirloom that had been in the Logan family for generation.

He'd read through the letter twice before the meaning sank in, but the words had remained branded in his memory.

> Jesse,
> I have nothing left to give. If I stay on the ranch, I'll never become the person I was meant to be. You were the one who wanted a family, so I'm leaving the babies with you. I'm going back to Kansas City and I'll contact you when I'm settled.
> Marie.

The storm bending the trees outside hadn't compared to the ones raging inside him.

Frantic, Jesse had immediately called the nurse's station in the Manhattan hospital where their premature triplets had been in the NICU for the past two months. The nurse had verified that Marie hadn't shown up that afternoon to sit with the girls.

He'd braved the weather to drive to the hospital anyway, hoping that his wife had had a change of heart and gone there instead of the airport.

She hadn't.

Jessie had stayed with his daughters the rest of the evening, waiting for a phone call. It wasn't until one of the nurses on duty had asked if his ranch was near High Plains that he'd learned about the tornadoes spawned by the storm.

Unable to get through to his hired hands or his sister Maya, Jessie had spent a sleepless night in the family lounge and most of the morning waiting for the state police to remove the barricades from the roads.

When he was finally able to return to the ranch, Jessie had gone from room to room calling Marie's name. Praying that news of the storm had fanned an ember of concern in her heart and brought her home. If not for him, then for Madison, Brooke and Sasha.

At the thought of his precious girls, Jesse was struck by an overwhelming desire to hold them again.

"I have to get back to the hospital." He pushed past Colt.

"Jessie…" Colt frowned.

Don't say it, Jesse thought. His self-control was hanging by a thread, but he couldn't think about his own grief. He had to think about the three babies he'd left sleeping peacefully in their cribs only a few hours ago. He had to keep it together. For his daughters.

As if Colt could read his mind, he nodded slowly. "I understand. And don't worry about the…arrangements right now, Jess. Take as much time as you need."

The automatic doors parted as Jesse reached the front of the building. He'd spent so much time at the hospital over the past eight weeks that many of the staff knew him by name. Two volunteer auxiliary works stopped talking and nodded solemnly when he passed the information desk. On emotional autopilot, he took the elevator to the NICU. When he reached the nursery, he heard someone singing softly to the girls.

But it wasn't his sister.

Sitting beside the crib where his daughters slept was Lori Martin, the young auburn-haired nurse he'd met once or twice. Jessie hadn't gotten to know her as well as he had the other nurses because her shift ended before he arrived to sit with the girls every evening.

The soft smile of Laurie's face and the expression in her eyes made Jesse's chest tighten.

It wasn't right.

Marie should have been the one singing to them. Loving them. And yet she'd left them…all of them.

Jesse's fists clenched at his sides.

Marie was gone, but he had three reasons to live. His daughters. And Jesse decided to make sure no one would hurt them again.

Love Inspired®
SUSPENSE
RIVETING INSPIRATIONAL ROMANCE

These contemporary tales
of intrigue and romance
feature Christian characters
facing challenges to their faith...
and their lives!

**Four new Love Inspired Suspense titles are
available every month wherever books are
sold, including most bookstores, supermarkets,
drug stores and discount stores.**

Steeple
Hill®

Visit:
www.steeplehillbooks.com

Love Inspired.
HISTORICAL
INSPIRATIONAL HISTORICAL ROMANCE

Engaging stories of romance,
adventure and faith,
these novels are set in
various historical periods
from biblical times
to World War II.

NOW AVAILABLE!

**Steeple
Hill**®

For exciting stories that reflect traditional values,
visit:
www.SteepleHill.com